2016

BEAR SEASON

Bernie Hafeli

Broken Bird Press
Portland, OR

Bear Season
© 2013 Bernie Hafeli

Published by Broken Bird Press
in association with *The Conium Review*
Portland, Oregon

ISBN-10 0982595654
ISBN-13 978-0-9825956-5-7

10 9 8 7 6 5 4 3 2 1

Author: Bernie Hafeli
Copy Editor: Holly Tri
Page Layout: James R. Gapinski
Cover Layout: James R. Gapinski & Uma Sankaram
Cover Image: Pernambuko, "Wojtek Soldier Bear," digital rendering, licensed under CC BY-SA 3.0

The author wishes to acknowledge, as a source, *Soldier Bear*, by Geoffrey Morgan and W.A. Lasocki (Armada Lions Press, 1972).

For Jinko.

Thanks for the nudge
and for everything.

BEAR SEASON

The summer had started badly. I'd just turned eleven and received a black eye as a gift from Jozef, my upstairs neighbor who was seven months older than I was. Every year around the time of my birthday Jozef made me understand that just because I was now his equal in years, I was still lagging woefully behind in the areas that really mattered: physical strength, popularity, and courage, along with its fellow attribute, manliness. Jozef, however, was hardly the best role model for someone in pursuit of these prized characteristics. For instance, how much courage did it take to beat up a skinny, underdeveloped kid like me? Was this the sort of thing I was supposed to emulate in order to claim that sought-after quality? And where did an eleven-year-old learn about manliness? From Superman? The Lone Ranger? The war movies on Saturday afternoons? Especially when the child never had a father, as was the case with me.

Well, not exactly the case. At one time I did have a father, as my mother and Uncle Izzy liked to point out. He'd died in the Battle of Monte Cassino during World

War II. This fact, of course, counted for nothing with the fat lout Jozef, who would sneer, "Stop sniveling, you dumb polak bastard," as his fists rained down on my hands, which uncourageously covered my face, even though I was no bastard and he was as Polish as I was. At Our Lady Queen of Martyrs, teachers called him *Yozef*, with a *Y*, while I was always the more Americanized Chester, even though my given name is Czeslaw. I also wasn't dumb; I regularly made the honor roll, something Jozef never did, and one of the reasons, I now believe, behind the seasonal pummellings. What made the beating that summer different than the others was that my uncle witnessed the tail end of it. Jozef had tripped me on the landing as I was leaving my uncle's flat, where I'd placed his laundry that my mother had washed and folded. Apparently, Jozef had been waiting for me in his own flat, located across from my uncle's, where my nemesis spent his time reading comic books and the "art" magazines that arrived for his father in plain brown wrappers. When he heard footsteps on the landing, he knew who it was—all the adults were either out working, or in the case of my uncle, drinking at Joe Dzirada's Bar—and he fell upon me with the pent-up gusto of a year's abstinence from bodily assault, at least as it pertained to me, grounding my cheek into the faded, flower-patterned carpet that smelled of pierogi, cabbage, kielbasa, and chicken soup.

"Happy birthday, Shit for Brains," he muttered in my ear, which was what he called me out of the earshot of others; and, I learned later, how his father liked to refer to him.

Maybe I should have been pleased he remembered

my birthday. But this was not my thought as he pounded my neck and the back of my head, voicing his displeasure at the fact I breathed the same air he did in our two-story brick dwelling. The building, at 111 Ellery Street in the shadow of the Dodge Main Plant, also housed his parents, my uncle, and my mother, but none of these people provoked Jozef's ire. Only me. Possibly he resented that my mother owned the building and felt this gave me some advantage over him. Or maybe it was because we had no dogs or cats to kick around. In any case, so intent was my antagonist on his work that he failed to hear the tread of my uncle coming up the stairs.

"Jozef! Jezus Christus!"

He pulled Jozef off me with such force that the body of my pudgy assailant slammed impressively against the wall, Jozef's head knocking a contour into the wallpaper that remained there as long as my mother owned the building. Immediately Jozef started to cry, an unexpected turn of events that gratified me for two reasons: one, it meant Jozef was in pain; two, crying was something I never did.

"Go wipe your face," my uncle said to my enemy.

Jozef, who was now whimpering, rose slowly to his feet and walked to the door of his family's flat, never once looking my way, unwilling to bear the heat of my castigating glare. Before disappearing inside, Jozef gave my uncle a cold, injured look, wondering, I suppose, what right a grown man had to bounce him off the hallway walls—a man other than his father that is. My uncle shook his head as Jozef's door clicked closed.

"I didn't mean to hurt him," he said.

"I'm glad you did."

"Don't say that, Czeslaw."

"But you saw what he did. He's a fat stupid shit."

My uncle held up one finger, then knelt before me on one knee, like an altar boy at Sunday Mass. His eyes were now level with mine, and his breath smelled of alcohol. "He's not a shit. He's a human being who sometimes acts like a shit." At the edges of his brown eyes, pink smears were bleeding into the whites. "The thing about human beings," he said, "is you don't always know why they do things. Sometimes bad things happen and it makes them behave in ways we don't like."

"But he has free will," I objected. I knew this was true. Sister Rosemarian had been apprising us of the fact since February—everyone had the choice to walk in Christ's footsteps, or, like Jozef, to fall prey to the ways of the flesh.

"It's not always so easy," my uncle said. He stood up and leaned backward from his heels until I heard his back crack. "What do you say we go up on the roof?" He was smiling now. "It's summer after all."

Once outside everything was better. Gone was the murk and fustiness of the house's interior, and with it some of the outrage of Jozef's unwarranted abuse, replaced by the freshness of an early summer afternoon. From our vantage point on the roof, the neighborhood spread out like splashed paint, more vivid closer in where smokestacks from the Dodge plant released a gray, not altogether unpleasant smelling vapor into the otherwise cloudless sky; and down below, at the corner, where the screen door to Joe Dzirada's Bar opened and closed with the flow of afternoon patrons. Farther off where Joseph Campau Street cut a swath through the rows of two- and three-story houses—and in the opposite direction where a freeway would soon be—the view was hazier, tinged with soot from the Dodge plant and the diffusion of sunlight and distance. Directly below us was my mother's garden, four square and two rectangular plots of flowers in every color—peonies, zinnias, daffodils, mums, roses, violets—that she tended every evening after arriving home from work, weeding, watering, fertilizing, moving plants from one bed to another, until the small backyard resembled, as much as it ever could, her mother's own garden in Poland. Between the flowerbeds were swaths of dark green grass that she wouldn't allow my uncle to cut; she insisted on doing it herself, nudging along the push mower on Saturday mornings before the temperature climbed too high, stopping to periodically swat at the incessant bees that were drawn to our yard as to a powerful narcotic.

Beyond the garden and its trellis of yellow roses stood the gate to the alley, a shadowy domain I was forbidden to enter unless accompanied by someone older. According to my mother, nothing good ever happened there. The branches of trees that overhung it and the profusion of untended bushes that spilled over from peoples' backyards provided the necessary cover for neighborhood hooligans to plot their petty crimes. High school dropouts cruised their souped-up coupes up and down its cinder tracks, trying to impress their girlfriends with their recklessness, and the neighbors with how little they cared about noise-restriction ordinances. Sometimes, late at night, my uncle could also be found there, drinking and passing the time with the three or four men who, along with Joe Dzirada, hadn't yet found his company objectionable. These men, like my uncle, were all veterans of World War II and they bore its scars, not so much in a physical sense, although Florin limped from a shrapnel wound near his knee, but in the way they now chose to connect, or not to connect, with the world. To say they wore the world like a loose garment gives them too much credit. For the most part, they tried to shuck it off completely, relying on alcohol and, in Florin's case, codeine, to do the trick. It was as if their eyes had been damaged and could no longer bear direct light; they had to narrow their eyelids and look at life from an angle, make things appear fuzzy in order to be okay with them. Post-traumatic stress disorder wasn't a term anyone used then. People just said you'd gone a little screwy or were messed up in the head.

Uncle Izzy was probably the worst. While the others could hold down jobs and muddle through family life, my uncle could manage neither. Since he'd arrived in Detroit, eight months was the longest he'd ever stayed employed, as a riveter at the Hamtramck Dodge plant four blocks away. He'd been given the job because of my mother, who worked with the wife of one of the foremen. Although technically never drunk on the job, Uncle Izzy was often hung over and would sometimes curl up for a nap on a wooden handcart before the next assembly line run of Wayfarers, Meadowbrooks, or Dodge Coronets. The foreman found him on that handcart once too often. My mother—who had learned English after coming from Poland, put herself through night school, and been hired as a researcher at Parke Davis—was livid.

"You have shamed us, Izydor! To them we're a family of drunks and deadbeats!"

My uncle's custom when she became angry was to clasp both hands together just below his waist and stare at the floor, like a contrite prisoner awaiting sentencing. This only served to infuriate her further.

"Look at me!"

She slapped him across the face.

He did as she said then, but not with an expression of shock or concern, which is what I felt at that moment— I'd never known my mother to use physical force. Instead, my uncle's eyes hardened in their familiar way and his lips settled into the bitter smirk that said: "Once again the world has chosen to piss on Izydor Wierzbicki. So glad not to be disappointed!"

"You're *dobre za nic*," my mother hissed, a phrase she used often that meant *good for nothing*, but sounded much worse in Polish. "You dishonor the memory of Aleksy."

Aleksy had been my uncle's brother and, though I couldn't call up even a single memory of him, my own father. Before the war, he and my uncle had been in the same Soviet gulag, and then served in the same company during World War II.

Behind me, my uncle's chair scraped the pebbles that covered the roof tar. Then I clearly heard the sound of a metal cap twisting against the swirled neck of a bottle. At Joe Dzirada's Bar, my uncle was a shot and a beer man, but alone he always drank vodka. When I turned to watch, he was sitting in one of the old dining room chairs my mother had given him, which he in turn had dragged up here. The chair was tilted back so his shoulders rested against the door to the stairwell, his feet inches off the ground, shoes off so the heel of one foot could rub the instep of the other. In the gulag he'd suffered from frostbite and sometimes his feet still tingled. In one hand he held a paperback book. On the cover a scantily clothed woman pointed a gun at her half-opened door. His other hand grasped the vodka. He seemed engrossed in the book, his lips in a frown, as he followed the fate of the redhead on the cover, or so I imagined. His limp black hair lay flat against his head, except in front where a cowlick caused it to spill over one eyebrow. He was thin, never regaining the weight he'd had before being sent to the gulag, and later to World War II. As usual, he had the beginnings of a beard; he shaved every third day, on an average. His clothes never fit; he bought them all secondhand, not wanting to blow money on anything less vital than booze. He was always pale. Sometimes after a particularly harsh night of drinking, his skin would carry a grayish cast. When he walked, it was with a limp, whether due to the frostbite or some other misfortune, I never determined. And in spite of an almost total disregard for how he looked, and for the impression he made on others, he was quite handsome, at least in my estimation; although according to my mother, my father was the more striking of the two. She had pictures of them both from the late 1930's; my father generally with a grin on his face; my uncle, the older son, looking more wary and serious, even dour. Sometimes in the afternoon when no one was home, I'd pull out those old pictures and try to comb my hair in the style they both favored back then in Poland—slicked back on the sides, fuller, and a bit wilder on top.

"Is that book any good?" I asked.

"Mmmm," my uncle muttered, not looking up, still rubbing his feet with enough force I could hear the fabric of one white sock brushing against the other.

"Do your feet itch?"

He nodded, still absorbed in the book. "It's the frostbite," he said. "A small price to pay considering what could have happened."

That was certainly true. My father had died, after all, when enemy shells overshot the front lines and exploded where Second Company was loading boxes of ammunition for the ongoing battle. Four others also lost their lives. Uncle Izzy, luckily, had been in another part of camp and escaped injury. In light of how his life had gone since that time, he considered it his final stroke of good luck.

Now my uncle lowered his book. "I'm sorry," he said.

"For what?"

"I didn't mean to bring up your father. I wasn't thinking."

"It's okay."

His eyes narrowed and he peered at me, alone with his thoughts; then he planted the vodka bottle among the roof pebbles. "Is something troubling you, Czeslaw?"

"Chester," I corrected.

"Are you still upset with Jozef?"

I wasn't sure why I was upset exactly, but the more I thought about it, I knew it had little to do with Jozef. I shook my head no.

"Then what?" My uncle smiled. "Ches-*ter*," he said, teasing me, annunciating each syllable. "Mister America."

The longer he smiled, the more I felt that I wanted to cry. But crying was something I refused to do. Instead I looked away, down at the pebbles covering the hardened roof tar. My uncle loved me; that much I knew. He just hadn't shown enough concern, I decided, to make up for the injustice I'd suffered at the hands of the bully Jozef. Instead of asking if I'd been hurt, he'd chided me for calling Jozef a shit. Then he'd come up here to drink and read his books, which is what he always did. It was how he contended with life; the world dealt you another blow, where was the surprise in that? You shrugged, went and found something to drink, lost yourself for a while in the pages of a book, and plodded on.

"Would you like a Wojtek story?" he asked.

Who wouldn't want a Wojtek story? Wojtek was a bear who had been the mascot of the Second Company during World War II, the company my father and my uncle had served in. I nodded my assent.

"Well," my uncle began, "this incident happened in the summer, during the *hamsin*. Do you know of the *hamsin*?"

I didn't and shook my head.

"What do they teach you in that school?"

I shrugged, waiting for him to continue. It was my uncle's contention that if the nuns at Our Lady Queen of Martyrs spent more time schooling us about the world and its many wonders, and less time filling our heads with the gospel of Christ, we'd all be better Christians—more intelligent Christians too.

Sighing, Uncle Izzy looked off at the smoke rising from the Dodge plant. It was white now, as if the autoworkers had elected a new pope.

"The *hamsin*," he explained, "is a hot dry wind that blows across Iraq each summer, raising great clouds of dust. It covers everything. And the heat is so intense it's impossible to touch the hood of a Jeep without wearing a glove. This presented a problem for Wojtek."

The problem was that Wojtek with his thick coat of fur didn't do well in the withering heat. So he took to spending long hours in the bathhouse, where he'd learned to pull the chain releasing the shower water. This soon led to his banishment from the baths, since he started monopolizing the soldiers' water. Then, one night as the company slept, Wojtek noticed the door to the bathhouse had been left slightly ajar. Not one to miss an opportunity, he padded over to the door, pushed it all the way open, and was greeted by a blood-chilling scream that awakened the entire camp. It turned out Wojtek had surprised an intruder, a scout for an Arab raiding party looking for weapons. The man had picked the lock to the bath hut hoping to find rifles, and instead had attracted the bear. The Arab was so terrified of Wojtek —the soldiers threatened to lock him in the bath hut with the bear—that he confessed everything. Based on his information, the members of his group were captured in a nearby village that evening.

For his efforts, Wojtek was rewarded with two bottles of beer, which he loved to drink, and a whole morning in the bathhouse.

"Then we gave him a cigarette," my uncle said. "A

Player's. He liked how the smoke smelled."

For the most part, I believed my uncle about Wojtek. He was my uncle, after all, and despite his failings, he wasn't a liar, not that I knew of anyway, at least not at that moment. But other people weren't quite so accepting. They saw the bear stories as evidence of delusional thinking, a mind that had been knocked clear off its moorings by the barbarity of war and unchecked drinking—another reason to avoid him at every cost. I suppose the image of Wojtek smoking cigarettes struck me as too outlandish, an unnecessary flourish that would only add fuel to the fire of his many detractors; not because he would fall any lower in their estimation, but because I might. Recently I had noted a change in how people reacted to me when I was in his company, no longer with commiseration and something approaching pity, but now with looks of puzzlement and even mild reproach, as if they couldn't understand how I could still believe in the Tooth Fairy.

"I don't believe you," I said.

He turned and looked at me then. "Come over here, Chester."

Reluctantly, I took the few steps that brought me closer to his chair. I'd never questioned his stories before.

"Have I ever lied to you?" he asked.

I looked in his eyes. There were flecks of orange in among the brown. Vodka scented his breath. If he had ever lied, the lies had been minor and inconsequential and I couldn't remember them. I shook my head no.

"Then why do you think I'm lying now?"

"I'm not *saying* you're lying."

His look softened somewhat. "Then what, Czeslaw?"

"Why would a bear ever smoke cigarettes?"

I just couldn't see it. I'd tried smoking the previous winter. After choking on the smoke, I'd coughed it up until my lungs felt like they'd been raked by red-hot pitchforks, and I was left gasping, wheezing, and drooling mucus. I couldn't imagine a bear enjoying something like that. Now my uncle started to smile.

"Wojtek didn't smoke cigarettes," he said. "He ate them."

"He ate cigarettes? Lit ones?" I found this equally hard to believe. But like many Wojtek stories, it began to feel like the truth; too preposterous to be made up.

My uncle was nodding, his smile widening. "No one could understand it. Piotr thought the smell of sweet tobacco reminded Wojtek of honeycombs."

Piotr had been Wojtek's special handler, assigned by the company commander once it was decided Wojtek would remain with the company. Piotr and my father first encountered Wojtek on a mountain road in what was then Persia, where they purchased the bear cub from a hungry native boy for two banknotes, an army knife, a chocolate bar, and a tin of meat.

To others, at least to those who believed my uncle's bear tales, I suppose the sale of the bear by the Persian boy was simply another Wojtek story, and not even the best one, but it was the story that affected my mother and me the most. It seemed to soften her, and sometimes could even bring her to tears; because of my father's involvement certainly, but also because of the boy, I think. Naturally, she knew I loved hearing about the bear, and I was only *hearing* about Wojtek; I hadn't been the one who found him wandering high up in the mountains as a tiny bear cub. She could only imagine how much that Persian boy must have loved that little bear, and how desperate and hungry he must have been to part with it.

"A chocolate bar," she would say with a shake of the head. "That poor boy."

"Cadbury's," my uncle would point out. "Pretty good chocolate."

"Don't joke, Izydor."

Then she always looked at me with such sadness it was as if I was the little Persian boy in tattered sandals, or as if she could imagine my life in similar straits: what might have happened, for instance, had she not taken all her savings and boarded a ship for America to live with her sister, bringing the fetal me with her?

"And the little boy cried?" If my uncle failed to mention this fact, she always asked.

"Yes, according to Aleksy. Until the boy started eating."

And here she would nod and look away, her eyes acquiring a faraway look, seeing again perhaps the way things had been over there, and probably still were.

But not over here, Mama, I wanted to tell her. *Here things are fine.* Which is what you learn quickly when the two people closest to you grew up in Poland on the eve of World War II.

"Someday you'll meet Wojtek," my uncle promised now, not for the first time.

This I had come to regard as wishful thinking. Wojtek now resided in the Edinburgh Zoo, and, to my knowledge, my uncle didn't have enough money to take us across the river to Canada, much less across the Atlantic Ocean to Scotland.

"Someday soon maybe," my uncle said. He stood up then and walked to the edge of the roof, facing the Dodge plant. "But first maybe we'll take a shorter trip."

Still watching the smokestacks, he asked, "Would you like to take a trip this summer?"

Suddenly I was so excited my skin tingled and it felt like my scalp went numb, until I realized this was my uncle speaking, who hadn't worked since Valentine's Day except for helping out Joe Dzirada on Saturday nights.

"Where?" I asked him, perhaps without the enthusiasm he would have liked.

"That way." He pointed at the Dodge plant. "The same direction as Scotland."

"Bob-Lo?" I asked, referring to the amusement park on the Detroit River where he took me every summer.

"No, not Bob-Lo." He turned to face me. "Cleveland," he said, deepening his voice to give that exotic destination the respect it deserved. "On the shores of Great Lake Erie."

The truth was I very much wanted to go. To someone who hadn't set foot outside metropolitan Detroit, except to visit his mother's farmer friends near Ypsilanti, Cleveland may as well have been Constantinople.

"Yes," I said. "I'd like to go."

In the next few weeks, we tried to win my mother's

endorsement for the idea of me accompanying my uncle to Cleveland. The campaign was fought on two fronts. First, my uncle thought it necessary to convince her of his own honorable intentions.

"I need to work," he told her. "It's not so easy here. I have a track record that raises flags with potential employers."

"And whose fault is that, Izydor?"

My mother was chopping carrots for chicken soup. For a moment, the only sound was the thonk-thonk-thonk of her knife on the cutting board.

"Entirely mine," my uncle said. "But a man can change, Ilona. And I am such a man."

My mother's head turned, and she regarded him coolly, then continued chopping.

"I just need a fresh start," he said. "In Cleveland, Bronislaw Wawryk can get me into the steel mills for interviews. I'll be back in ten days."

"In Cleveland they won't care about your employment history in Detroit?" My mother said this without looking at him. By now she'd moved from carrots to celery.

"Maybe not so much." My uncle put his hands in his pockets. "Anyway, they don't have to know. I can say I just arrived form some foreign place."

"This is an example of how you've changed?"

My uncle opened his mouth, then closed it and looked at me. "Your mother doesn't miss a trick, Czeslaw. There is much you can learn from her. I hope you pay attention."

Then he left the kitchen.

But my uncle hadn't given up, and over the next few

weeks my mother relented somewhat to the idea that he was seeking honest employment and was in fact a changed man. It didn't hurt that Bronislaw Wawryk called to validate my uncle's story. My mother remembered Bronislaw from the village of Zielonki, outside Krakow, where they'd all grown up at a time and in a place that must have seemed like the Middle Ages when viewed from Detroit in 1951. Nor did it hurt that my uncle was paying for his exploratory trip. My mother and I were both flabbergasted to learn that for years Uncle Izzy had been jamming dollar bills down the necks of old vodka bottles until he'd saved enough for roundtrip Greyhound tickets to places well beyond Cleveland. When he showed me the bottles, there were red and blue-colored bills at the bottom that were British and Scottish pounds; he must have started saving them during or just after the war.

With things going well on this front, my uncle took the offensive on the second front of our campaign to win my mother's blessings, which was to convince her that my going with him to Cleveland was a really good idea. For this, he needed my help. One night after dinner, he wanted me to bring my old globe into the living room where my mother liked to sit on the sofa reading *The Detroit News*, her one moment of respite after working all day at Parke Davis, then preparing and disposing of dinner, and then restoring order to the garden. His plan was for me to lie on my stomach on the floor and spin the globe on its axis, watch morosely as it completed its series of revolutions, and when it stopped, to look out the window and sigh. This I did a number of times before my mother lowered her paper and frowned.

"What's the matter, Chester?"

"Poor kid," my uncle said. "He's never been anywhere."

My mother looked at him and went back to the evening paper.

"You know when I was his age," my uncle went on, "I'd been all over—Lodz, Lublin, Krakow, Ostrava."

This had no effect on my mother. While she remained absorbed in her paper, I tried to read what was on the back page. There was probably a Hudson's ad for inflatable swimming pools and a story about families leaving Detroit for the suburbs; it was a common talking point that summer. Except for cars driving by the open window, everything was quiet.

Then my uncle said, "Hey, I have an idea." He may have even slapped his thigh. "Why don't I take Czeslaw to Cleveland?"

Again the newspaper lowered. This time there was a look on my mother's face I had never encountered, a mixture of the aspects of disbelief—confusion, shock, horror, concern—all directed at my uncle and the fact his reasoning powers had deteriorated to such a state that he could make such an absurd, poorly conceived, completely objectionable suggestion.

"Just think about it, Ilona. For the boy's sake."

"For the boy's sake?" By now my mother had regained the ability to speak, and at a decibel level higher than before. "Are you crazy? Have you pickled your brain with vodka?"

When she stood up, the paper scattered over the floor. "For the boy's sake I should throw you out on the street, before you do him serious damage!"

She started pacing back and forth in front of the sofa, stepping on the fallen newspaper, first looking at the carpet, then throwing her head back in an auburn wave so she could stare at the ceiling.

"Let me understand this," she said. "My drunken brother-in-law who can't hold a job for more than two months, unless it's as a bartender; who spends more time on the bench in front of the five-and-dime than the pigeons do; who, when they see him in time, people cross the street in order to avoid, unless they're policemen; this man wants me to trust him with the responsibility of my only son on a trip to Cleveland?"

A smile formed on her lips, still bright with the lipstick she wore to the research lab every day. It was a mirthless smile. In his chair, my uncle sat stone-faced until her final words finished ringing off the glass and metal furnishings. Then he smiled too.

"Ilona," he said. "You will have nothing to worry about. I will quit drinking."

"Ha!"

"Starting Sunday."

This was a Thursday. Saturday night he was tending bar for Joe Dzirada. My mother only shook her head, still smiling to herself, then walked from the room, through the kitchen, her footsteps snapping across the old linoleum. Her bedroom door slammed.

My uncle looked at me. "Don't worry," he said, lifting his thumb in the air. "We'll win."

I don't know if he actually quit drinking. I do know that over the entire month of July, whenever I came close enough to sniff out the aftershave he wore or the lingering scent of cigars and cigarettes he smoked, never once did I notice alcohol. His stretch of alleged sobriety started impressively, with a performance reminiscent of a silent movie. Sunday morning, as my mother stood by the sink drying the breakfast dishes, my uncle thudded down the backstairs, entering our kitchen with a large seaman's bag perched on his shoulder. Without a word, he emptied the sack on the kitchen floor, sending bottles of different shapes and sizes clattering over the linoleum. Most of the alcoholic spirits were represented, but the majority were vodka bottles. He then poured the contents of each bottle—if there were any contents, most of the bottles were already drained—into the sink, then placed the bottle back in his sack, each additional bottle producing a louder, more resounding *clink!* When he finished, he hoisted the bag back over his shoulder and stomped out of the kitchen to the backstairs, bringing to mind a thinner, more desperate Santa Claus. "Ho, ho, ho!" he said as he left, reinforcing the strange Santa association.

If my mother wasn't moved by Uncle Izzy's efforts, I was. At that age I didn't understand the attraction of alcohol. The few times I'd sampled it, the result had been akin to my first taste of tobacco: I coughed and gagged as my body instinctively rejected the offending substance, sending it back up my throat and out my mouth and nose as I wondered how anyone could enjoy anything so vile. I counted it as one of the mysteries of growing up. At a certain age, apparently, a molecular change would occur in my body that made cigarettes preferable to hot apple pie, and vodka more appealing than a chocolate malt. Because this had certainly happened to my uncle, hadn't it? Until that July, his pursuit of alcohol had been absolute, relegating everything else, including his relationship with my mother, and even with me, to the periphery. Once he stopped drinking though, or at least so relentlessly, it was as if a great gulf opened up that had previously been flooded with alcohol. He needed to fill it with something and since he wasn't working regularly, and wasn't involved with any women that I knew of, and had no outside interests other than reading pulp detective stories, he chose to fill the hole with me. I was thrilled. I placed a great deal of emphasis on time spent with Uncle Izzy. Because my father had died, my uncle's attention meant more than it otherwise would have. Even at his drunkest I think he could sense this; and because he was at heart a kind man, he tried to accommodate me. He took me for ice cream at the soda shop down the block and to the five-and-dime on Joseph Campau Street. He took me to the library and the fire station; he knew the afternoon librarian, some of the firemen, and Rudy the firehouse dog. But mostly he took me up on the roof or to Joe Dzirada's Bar. There it felt the most like father and son. We simply spent time in each other's company. If he wanted to read: great. If he wanted to drink, that was fine too. The only uncomfortable moments were at the bar when he started to talk about Wojtek. If no one was at our table, then there wasn't a problem; but if someone, even one of his band of veterans, happened to be present, I would feel myself tense up at the first mention of the bear, and would glance away from the bottle of Vernor's ginger ale and bag of Better Made potato chips my uncle always bought me to see if I could detect the first smirk, yawn, or raised eyebrow I knew would come from whoever was being enlightened by my uncle. That July, however, there was no longer an issue. With his wits about him, my uncle was unlikely to bring up the bear at Joe Dzirada's Bar. He could tell that it bothered me.

But there were other benefits of my uncle's unaccustomed spell of levelheadedness. One evening when we climbed up to the roof, I discovered a telescope had been set up there, angled on its tripod in the opposite direction of the lowering sun.

"Where'd that come from?" I asked him.

"It was your father's and mine. When we were kids. It was in the bottom of my closet. I forgot it was there."

"Can I look?"

"Of course. That's why it's up here." He put one eye to the telescope and aimed it at the first star to pierce the blue and purple sky. For a minute he fiddled with the focus. "Have a look," he said.

At first I saw nothing but a field of beige.

"Don't squint. Look at it like it's a pear sitting on a table."

I relaxed my eye and immediately saw a circle of pure white, glittering in the dark. Near the bottom, a scallop was covered in shadow, making it appear as if a part of the surface had fallen in.

"The evening star," my uncle said. "Also known as Venus."

I adjusted the focus as he had done, only to return to his original setting. "Why do they call it a star if it's a planet?"

"The poets saw it first. They thought it was a star. The planets weren't conceived of yet."

"How can you tell the difference?" I moved away from the telescope. Knowing the answer seemed important.

My uncle shrugged. "Do I look like an astronomer?"

In a few minutes another star or planet made its appearance. Again Uncle Izzy went to the telescope and played with the focus. "Take a look," he said.

It wasn't as bright as Venus; it appeared bluer and colder, but it was round and it glowed.

"That's Vega," he said. "A star, not a planet."

"But how do you know?"

"Somebody told me. Now I'm telling you."

I stepped back from the telescope. My uncle was slouched back in his chair now, staring up at Vega, a speck of light that had grown infinitely more interesting once a name was attached to it.

"Our father instructed us in the stars of the night sky," he said. "For awhile Aleksy wanted to be an astronomer."

This was new information. Why hadn't I been told? Suddenly astronomy seemed like the most worthwhile subject a boy could pursue. I scanned the evening sky until I recognized the Big Dipper, which was the limit of my knowledge as far as astronomy went.

"Let's look at the Big Dipper," I said.

With a grunt, my uncle stood up from his chair to oblige. "In Great Britain," he said, "they call it the Plough."

With this knowledge, I gazed through the lens at the pattern of stars. To me they still looked like an enormous dipper, not at all like a plough.

"It's part of Ursa Major," Uncle Izzy added. "The Great Bear. Because early stargazers thought it looked like one."

"The poets?" I asked.

"Somebody ancient and Greek."

I glanced at him and he smiled. When I peered through the telescope again, twisting the knob for a wider field of vision, the stars blurred then gradually came into focus, like lights at night through a rainy windshield.

"There's a legend that goes with it. Do you want to hear?"

"Sure."

"It involves the most lecherous of gods—Zeus."

I wasn't sure what *lecherous* meant, only that it had to do with sex, a subject my mother was loath to mention but my uncle was sometimes willing to discuss.

"Zeus lusted, shall we say, after a nymph named Callisto."

When my uncle paused, I knew he was looking at me even though my right eye was trained on the star at the furthest tip of the Big Dipper, and my left eye was closed.

Uncle Izzy continued: "His wife Hera found out and in her anger turned Callisto into a bear. When Callisto's son, who was out hunting, came upon his mother as a bear, he nearly shot her with his arrow, but Zeus averted tragedy by reaching down and sweeping them both into the sky, where they became the constellation Ursa Major."

"That's hard to believe."

"It's an abbreviated version."

"But who would believe that? I thought the Greeks were smart."

"It's a myth. Myths are always hard to believe."

I looked at him. He was sitting in his chair again, minus his shoes, rubbing his feet together. Above him hung the July moon, looking like a perfectly round Communion wafer that would become the body and blood of Our Lord Jesus Christ.

"Like some of your Wojtek stories," I said.

He turned to me, about to speak, then changed his mind.

"Yes," he said after a moment. "I suppose."

"But the Wojtek stories are true?"

He shrugged and at the same time nodded, then held his hand out flat to the roof and wobbled it slightly from side to side, like a canoe in turbulent water. "Sometimes I enhance."

"If you had photographs, more people would believe you."

It had always seemed odd to me: a bear lived with a company of soldiers for three years and no one took pictures? Why didn't my uncle have any photos?

"I *had* photographs," Uncle Izzy said. "Someone else has them now." Sighing, he leaned forward in his chair, planting his shoeless feet among the roof pebbles. "When I was a sailor, I overindulged one night and passed out in a bar—in Marseilles. When I came to, all my pictures were gone, along with all my francs."

This had the earmarks of truth. One afternoon last fall I'd been with him when he passed out in Joe Dzirada's Bar, listening to the Lions' game.

"Were there pictures of my father?"

"A few."

My father and Wojtek. All the soldiers loved that bear, but Wojtek had enjoyed a special affinity with my father, who had been with him since the first minute; and, unlike Piotr, Wojtek's handler, hadn't had to lay down the law when Wojtek misbehaved, which was often, especially when the bear was a cub. After receiving a reprimand from Piotr, Wojtek would seek out my father for assurance that Wojtek was still loved despite whatever penance Piotr had administered, which by the time it was dispensed must have seemed confusing to the bear, who had probably forgotten what he'd done to earn it. According to my uncle, Wojtek was never disappointed when he ran to my father, who was very good at making Wojtek feel loved.

"Did he talk about me?"

My uncle looked at me. "Aleksy?"

"No, Wojtek."

Uncle Izzy contorted his face like he was trying to remember something that was proving difficult. "I remember your father talking about your mother, all the time, and about our family and friends in Zielonki, but—"

Here he pretended to concentrate even harder.

"—no, I don't think he ever mentioned a son named Chester."

"Czeslaw."

"No Czeslaw either."

"You're kidding." This was our routine.

"Of course he talked about you," my uncle said then. "He couldn't stop talking about you. You were his greatest joy." Now my uncle grinned. "It was his fervent hope that the three people who mattered most to him in the world would someday meet: you, your mother, and Wojtek."

I felt the familiar rush that always accompanied these words from my uncle—first cool and tingly, like I'd jumped off a dock into Lake St. Clair, then warm, like the water had heated to bath tub temperature.

"But Wojtek isn't a person," I said.

"He was to us."

"Tell me a story."

He was staring at his feet. Again a smile formed on his lips; not what you'd call a happy smile. "With or without enhancements?"

"I'm sorry if I hurt your feelings."

"Did you know that given half a chance Wojtek might have become an alcoholic?" When he looked at me I said nothing. I'd said enough already. "Like me?" he added.

"You're not an alcoholic."

This he waved off, as though the words were so much smoke. "I told you Wojtek liked to drink beer, didn't I?"

"Yes."

"Well he enjoyed more than beer. Anytime he saw someone with a bottle of alcohol, no matter what kind, he would beg for a taste, and more often than not he got one."

It was due to the bear's antics, my uncle explained, that soldiers were so willing to buy Wojtek a drink.

Grasping the offered bottle tightly in his paws, he would roll onto his back and pour the beverage down his throat. When the bottle was empty, he held it up to his eye and peered into the opening, hoping to find something left. After enough alcohol, he behaved like many humans under similar circumstances; he became happier and more daring. In Wojtek's case this often meant indulging in his favorite sport, which was wrestling. Standing up on his hind legs, he would wave his front paws in a dog-paddling type motion, inviting soldiers to a friendly fight. Anyone with no knowledge of Wojtek would simply steer clear. But if the soldier knew Wojtek well enough and was up to the challenge, then the members of the Second Transport Company were in for a treat. The match would generally start with the challenger moving in on Wojtek and pummeling the bear's chest with his fists. This would cause Wojtek to roar with delight until he succeeded in wrapping the man in a bear hug and forcing him down to the ground. Once on top of the soldier, Wojtek would slowly lower his large head, sticking his muzzle in the man's face. Baring his fangs, the bear then emitted a menacing growl, which his captive—who, despite having seen this before, couldn't help being alarmed now that it was happening to him—was forced to endure until Wojtek lost interest and set the man free, usually with a hot wet lick from his rough, aromatic tongue.

Of course Wojtek's drinking had its consequences too. After indulging, he was prone to suffering excruciating headaches. Drawn by his woeful moans, the men might find Wojtek near the cookhouse secured by a short chain to an iron peg—his punishment for drunkenly plundering the storeroom of his favorite foods—where he would be holding his head with both paws, as if it were a watermelon and if he just squeezed hard enough, the pain, like juice, would ooze away.

When my uncle finished his Wojtek story, he crossed his legs at the ankles, tilted back in his chair, and stared up at the constellation the British call the Plough.

"Why did they put up with Wojtek?" I asked him.

"Who?"

"The officers in charge. He caused so much trouble."

The wind had shifted and you could smell the Dodge plant—fetid, musty, on the verge of being offensive. It reminded me of the laboratory where my mom worked.

"You have to understand," my uncle said, "how terrible life was then." He turned to where I'd taken a seat—on the roof surface next to his chair, my back against an air vent. "It wasn't like now, when all you have to worry about is where to find a job, or maybe a wife, or someone to buy you a drink. Not like America." He shook his head, frowning. "People died—horribly—for no good reason."

Like my father, I thought, but knew better than to mention it to my uncle. It would only end our conversation.

"Hate was epidemic, more deadly than typhus. 'The rough beast's hour had come round at last.'" He smiled then. "You didn't know I quoted poetry."

"No."

"'Let us go then, you and I,'" he threw out his arm in a sweeping gesture, "'when the evening is spread out against the sky.'"

"You didn't answer my question."

Standing up from his chair, he looked in the direction of the Dodge plant, then leaned backward from his heels, stretching. "It was a bad time, Czeslaw. No fun to be had anywhere. When Piotr and your father bought the bear from the Persian boy, we all saw a chance for a bit of relief. He was only a cub then." When he stopped stretching, my uncle began pacing around the roof, slowly, following its perimeter like a sentry on guard duty, although a sentry with his hands in his pockets. "By the time the sergeant found out we had him, we'd grown quite attached to Wojtek. Of course the sergeant could see this. He liked how Wojtek had improved our morale. We decided to approach Major Chelminski and suggest Wojtek become the company mascot."

My uncle stopped near the corner of the roof closest to the Dodge plant. From where I sat, I couldn't actually see the factory but I knew what he was looking at: a hulking gray fortress topped with tall black smokestacks, as if the largest freight ship in the history of the world had sailed down the St. Lawrence Seaway, crossed Lake Ontario then Lake Erie, then cruised up the Detroit River and gone out of control, smashing into the bank and juggernauting forward, block after city block, until it finally stopped at the border of Detroit and Hamtramck. Billowing from its stacks, smoke darker than the night sky created clouds like moon shadows, and in certain windows lights blazed as welders welded, riveters riveted, and on the lower levels foundry workers poured hot molten metals into moulds for axles and engine parts. During the war the plant had manufactured military vehicles. My uncle, when he worked there, had spent his nights sweating in the foundry.

"The major agreed immediately," my uncle said, his eyes still on the factory. "He knew that the difference between victory and defeat is often slim. Everyone was looking for an edge. In his mind, Wojtek gave us one. Caring for him, playing with him brought up the same emotions we felt for the people we held dear. Love. Compassion. A desire to nurture and protect." Uncle Izzy turned to look at me. "Your father couldn't share his affection with you, so he made do with Wojtek. He was so close to the bear because he wanted to be close to you and your mother, even though he couldn't be. That was one reason at least."

My uncle returned to his chair and sat down. The wood groaned under his weight. "And Wojtek loved us back," he said. "I don't know what his life was like before he met us, but he was certainly grateful for our attention. You couldn't help but see it." He looked at me then. "Does that answer your question?"

I told him it did.

"He reminded us of Poland," Uncle Izzy went on, "before the Nazis and Stalin. He made us happy and the major could see that. So he added Wojtek's name to the roll of the Second Transport Company, and Wojtek officially became the hairiest of Allies."

"What rank?"

"Lance-mascot, Second Transport Company, Polish Army Service Corps."

In the darkness I doubt if my uncle could see me frown. Just my silence though, broken finally by the rumble of a car passing by on Ellery Street, was enough for him to amend his claim. "Actually Wojtek had no rank. Soldier bear we called him." He turned to look down at me. "And that's the truth, Czeslaw. You wouldn't think a group of men intent on the bloody annihilation of their fellow human beings could be capable of such enlightened thinking—in regard to keeping Wojtek I mean."

With his final words his voice trailed off, as if he were speaking only for his own benefit, annunciating his thoughts to see if he really agreed with them.

"Maybe that's why I miss it." He looked at the Dodge plant again. "Pretty sad, isn't it, a man who misses the Second World War?"

Reaching down, he scooped up a handful of roof gravel. "I have dreams of those days, and when I wake up I'm happy. Not like that damn place," he said, motioning with his head in the direction of the factory. Then he flung the stones, as if they might hit the Dodge plant. Of course none of them made it; the factory was blocks away. Instead I heard them rattle off the shingles of the Piotrowski's garage, some sounding sharper and more resonant when they collided with the Piotrowski's Buick.

"Let's go inside," he said. "It's time for the fights."

He referred to the Friday Night Fights, which we watched every week with Jozef and his parents—not the fights between Jozef's parents, which were less regular and not as entertaining. Since the Dudeks owned one of only three televisions on our block, all differences were put aside for the time it took the boxers to try to hammer one another into submission, punctuated by the earliest televised commercials for Stroh's beer, Gillette blue blades, and the cigars of R.G. Dun.

I still remember who won that night: Sugar Ray Robinson in a TKO.

The next day, as part of the ongoing campaign to win over my mother, my uncle cleaned out the cellar and hauled the refuse to the dump in Joe Dzirada's truck. In his absence, having nothing better to do on a warm, lazy, lingering Saturday afternoon, I decided to peek in his closet to see what other treasures might be hidden there besides the telescope. A chemistry set would have been nice, or a Ouija board like the Dudeks had, but I was especially hoping for something pertaining to my father: a box of misplaced photos perhaps, or some old report cards if they even used those in Zielonki, or a book with an inscription in flowing Polish script, signed *Aleksy*. I found plenty of books, mostly the paperback crime stories Uncle Izzy favored, with titles like *Pick Up on Noon Street* and *Love Can Be Murder*. The hardcovers were almost exclusively in Polish, and the ones that looked like they might bear an inscription—well, they didn't. I picked through stacks of folded clothes I'd never seen him wear, including old army uniforms. There was a dartboard with darts; a chess set with all the pieces; a rusty horseshoe—if it was supposed to bring luck, it hadn't been very effective in Uncle Izzy's case. In the corner were four cigar boxes, which seemed promising at first, but each one contained only bar paraphernalia: coasters, napkins, swizzle sticks, drink umbrellas, bottle openers from places like *Le Cochon Bleu, Caramba*, and *The Seven Sins Lounge*. All of this was stacked on top of a large travel trunk secured by a copper padlock. There were also collections of letters and postcards bound together with twine; I was tempted to untie them and take a look but everything was covered with a fine sprinkling of dust and I was afraid Uncle Izzy might notice they'd been tampered with. They seemed too personal for that, like I'd be sneaking a glimpse of someone's meaningful secrets, the thoughts they'd felt strongly enough to put into words, even though most of the writing would have been in Polish, which except for a few basic words, I wouldn't have understood anyway. Then, tucked between the trunk and the wall, I noticed a brown leather satchel. Rectangular in shape, it was slightly taller than a suitcase and much thinner; its odd dimensions drew me. When I pulled it out and laid it on my uncle's bed, there were scuffs in the leather and the corners were so frayed you could poke a finger all the way through. Even before I unfastened the brass snaps, I knew something important lived inside.

Sketches, it turned out. There must have been thirty in all, pencil drawings on thick, coarse sketch sheets the color of newspaper. I took my time leafing through them. He'd drawn a barn and a farmhouse, a horse, a pig, and a dog. Then there were faces of a man and a woman; my grandparents, I wondered? Then a boy, a fairly handsome boy, who I thought looked a bit like me; I put this picture aside. Next came drawings of a girl, a young woman perhaps; there were four of these and she was good looking, at least the artist had presented her that way.

All the sketches seemed very professional, realistically rendered, with a subtle whimsy in the length of a nose, the tangled mass of the girl's long hair. My uncle had mentioned he'd sometimes done drawings of people in bars in exchange for drinks, and that sometimes those caricatures had led to fights, but to actually discover the existence of these sketches was thrilling. The deeper I went into the collected drawings, the better and more detailed they became. Now people were in uniform, my uncle's war buddies. I thought I recognized my father. Where was everyone now? Who was the man with the black eyebrows and moustache? The next drawing was of Wojtek. I studied it closely; in it Wojtek was still a cub, licking the fingers of the man with the black moustache. In the next sketch, the man I thought might be my father was feeding Wojtek from a baby bottle. Then Wojtek was licking the nose of a Dalmatian. Then playing with a monkey. In fact, all the remaining pictures were of Wojtek: eating pie from a plate, wrestling with soldiers, riding in a Jeep, drinking beer, loading artillery boxes, standing on the deck of a ship. Why hadn't my uncle shared these with me? Or with his critics at the bar? No one would doubt the existence of the bear after seeing these drawings. I left them spread over his bed so he'd know that I'd found them, thinking it would lead to an explanation. But for weeks he said nothing. It was like the time I spent in his bedroom that muggy afternoon hadn't happened at all, as though I'd been lulled to sleep and dreamed everything up; created my own Wonderland.

Not long after our night of stargazing, my mother consented to let me go with my uncle to Cleveland. No doubt the weeks of his curtailed drinking had chipped away at her deep-rooted objections; and with his abstinence had come changes in my uncle's behavior that had been unthinkable a few short weeks before. Every night, for instance, he now helped with the evening dishes. During the day, while she was at work, he did all the accumulated laundry, including sheets, blankets, and tablecloths. He also weeded and watered her garden, and even cut the back lawn, which she had formerly forbid him to do. And in the evening, after the dishes were dried and put away, he swept the front porch, the front steps, the walkway and sidewalks, sometimes doing the Piotrowski's sidewalks for good measure.

Then, one evening, he spoke the magic words. "Ilona," he said, "if you allow Chester to come with me to Cleveland, he can visit your Uncle Jakub."

To say my mother adored Great Uncle Jakub barely scratched the fenders. Back in Poland, he'd helped raise her after her own father had died in the salt mines. The four times I could remember that he'd come to visit us in Detroit, she'd assumed the identity of another person— the mother I'd always hoped she might be. Her hard edges melted away and a lingering smile gave her face an unaccustomed look. Since Great Uncle Jakub was like a parent to her, he must have carried the whole dense web of associations that put her in touch with a more innocent time. She seemed to delight in just being near him: making sure he was warm enough, bringing him one of my father's old sweaters, preparing him chicken soup or pressure-cooked kielbasa. After a few hours in his presence, her accent grew thicker. Here was the girl who'd gone into the forest with him, collecting berries and wild mushrooms, who'd helped him with the frothy pails after milking the cows before sunrise.

"Okay, Izydor, you win. You can take Chester to Cleveland."

I couldn't quite believe what I'd heard. Up to now, the whole idea of going to Cleveland had felt like most of my uncle's other grand plans. Although they sounded good initially, putting them in action generally revealed serious flaws that prevented their ever reaching fruition.

But not this time. This time I was going to Cleveland.

"Thank you, Mama," I said. I couldn't remember ever being happier—maybe as a six-year-old on Christmas Eve.

"I'll miss you, Chester. You must promise to call and send many postcards. I'll pin them up on the kitchen wall."

I never questioned her love, but there were times, sometimes whole chilly months, when it seemed to lay dormant, like her garden beneath the winter snow. She was not ever what you'd call a happy woman, although she did seem happy at that moment.

"I promise, Mama."

"Come here. Let me hold you."

It must have slipped her mind that I was eleven now, too old for that. But it was a small price to pay compared to the misgiving she must have felt turning me over to my uncle. I went to her and she hugged me. For long, uncomfortable seconds I smelled her hairspray and facial powder and felt the softness of her cheek; it was always a mystery what do with my hands, but in less than a minute the ordeal was over.

"Next," my uncle said, "maybe you'll let me take him to meet Wojtek."

At these words I held my breath. Immediately my mother looked at me and there was something about my expression—perhaps the fact it screamed: *Yes! I'll do anything!*—that made her smile.

"It's a possibility," she said. "Maybe I'll let you take me along too."

My uncle glanced at me then, and we both looked at my mother. She must have known—my uncle had to have told her—that this would be the fulfillment of my late father's wish.

"Maybe when Chester finishes his first year of high school," she said, turning back to the kitchen counter and the preparation of dinner. "*If* he gets good grades."

It wasn't until the Sunday before we left that I learned the true reason for my uncle's Cleveland journey. The afternoon was sweltering, too stifling in my uncle's estimation to do anything but walk to the corner and immerse ourselves in the murk and relative cool of Joe Dzirada's Bar.

Halfway there, though, my uncle stopped. "We need to talk," he said.

Leaning against Leo Lewicki's DeSoto, which was parked at the curb in the shade of a tree so the metal wasn't too hot, my uncle fixed me with the look he reserved for the most serious matters, not a look he used often.

"You discovered my drawings," he said.

I nodded, finally busted; I felt relief.

"I thought it was Jozef. I've caught him in there before. But I asked him this morning and he had nothing to do with it."

The Dudeks had been on vacation. Every summer they went up north to Caseville, where a relative owned a fudge stand near the shores of Lake Huron. The weekend I found my uncle's sketches was the same weekend they'd driven up. They had returned the previous evening.

"Never did I imagine it was you," my uncle said, his eyes looking through me. "I thought you were more honest."

The criticism stung. In the weeks of wondering why he'd kept the drawings hidden, hadn't mentioned them even after I'd scattered them over his bed, I'd lost track of the fact I'd violated his privacy.

"I thought you'd know it was me," I said. "That's why I left them on the bed."

"But you said nothing."

I looked away from his x-ray eyes.

"You knew it was wrong. That's why you didn't tell me," he said.

"I didn't know what to say."

"But you knew it was wrong, right Czeslaw?"

I couldn't look at him. I nodded my head. After a moment I heard him sigh.

"It's all right," he said. "You only behaved like a human

being."

A police car went by. Slowing at the corner across from the bar, it stopped and waited at the entrance for a while, then turned left without using a blinker.

"Why didn't you show me your drawings?"

"What for? They aren't any good." When I looked at him he shrugged.

"They are good. I love them."

He glanced at me then, as if trying to gauge my sincerity. "Thank you," he said after a bit.

"Is that boy my father?"

"Yes. I was saving it for you. I was thinking of getting it framed."

"I'd love that."

"Okay, then." He smiled. "That's one Christmas present taken care of."

"What about the pictures of Wojtek?"

"You want those too?"

"They're good. You should show them to people."

He laughed. "Oh, I've shown them, all right. I stopped after my Wojtek photographs were stolen. Didn't want to lose the drawings too, whether they're good or not."

"They're good," I said.

"If you say so."

What I really wanted him to do was show the sketches in Joe Dzirada's Bar. Then everyone would believe him about the bear. Well, not everyone. For some, it might be just more evidence of what an oddball he was, the kind that did detailed drawings of an imaginary bear. But I thought more people would believe him. In fact, I had hopes someone might take a real interest and want to do an article or book using the drawings to illustrate, although Joe's wouldn't be the kind of place to pursue a thing like that. It would be more likely for Batman to walk through Joe's door than a writer or a book publisher.

"Have you shown the drawings to anyone here?" I asked him.

"In Detroit?" Uncle Izzy looked at me for what seemed a long time. "Yes," he said finally, "to Joe. He liked them. He even set up a meeting with an interested party."

"What happened?" I couldn't believe he'd never mentioned this fact.

"He wasn't interested."

"Oh."

"The interested party I mean. You'll have to ask Joe. I'm hazy on the details."

"Okay."

"Let's go. It's hot."

We walked on to Joe's. Inside there was no air conditioning yet, but Joe had three ceiling fans, plus assorted others strategically placed around the blue-tiled floor, that created enough stir in the dense air to generate a breeze, although not a cool breeze; compared to the furnace outside, it was at best lukewarm. My uncle and I claimed two of the swiveling barstools with cracked black leather seats. When I was younger, I liked to climb up on these stools and spin in circles, seeing how long I could go before the faces of people grew blurred and distorted, became funhouse images, until a queasiness took hold of my stomach and compelled me to stop. Later, I learned that the spinning I did back then bore certain similarities to getting drunk.

Joe Dzirada waved at us from the far end of the bar, where he was talking to a man called Stump. Draped over Joe's shoulder was the dishtowel he was never without, spotted with whiskey stains, drops of Eastern European liqueurs and wines, splotches of pickled egg and maraschino cherry. From the Philco radio behind the bar, Paul Williams and Ty Tyson announced the Tiger game from Briggs Stadium—in Corktown, not too far away. I listened closely for the latest exploits of George Kell, Johnny Groth, and especially my hero, Dick Kryhoski. In a back corner stood the jukebox, with its sleek curved tubes of pink and purple light. Affixed to the wall above the jukebox was a sort of miniature bandstand, roughly the size of an orange crate. When someone inserted a nickel in the jukebox and the first strains of "Tic-Toc Polka," "My Girlfriend Julayda," or "Hoop-Dee-Doo" began filling the barroom, the curtains of the small bandstand separated and a pint-sized polka band swung into action, the brightly painted doll musicians in perfect time to the buoyant, pumping music. The effect wasn't as impressive when a non-polka tune was selected, however; the accordions and clarinets felt out of place if someone played "Cold, Cold Heart" by Tony Bennett, or "Red Sails in the Sunset," or, as Stump had been doing all afternoon, "Cry" by Johnnie Ray.

After we'd been sitting a while, Florin and Gus, two of the people who still had time for my uncle, wandered in and found seats at the opposite end of the bar.

"I need to talk to them," Uncle Izzy said. "Will you be okay?"

"Yes."

"Joe will be here in a few minutes."

With that my uncle stood up and sauntered over to join Florin and Gus. In his absence I listened to Virgil Trucks walk the bases loaded and give up a double to Ferris Fain before Stump realized Johnnie Ray was no longer singing his favorite song and stood up to feed the jukebox. As he did so, Joe Dzirada started making his way in my direction, stopping to pluck a bag of Better Made potato chips from the rack and grab an empty glass and a bottle of Vernor's ginger ale.

"How's the boy?" Joe asked, placing the refreshments before me.

"I'm good." I didn't want to look him in the eye, hoping to avoid the inevitable.

"Once for good luck?"

He was smiling now, practically leering. The flesh wrinkled around his watery blue eyes; his doughy nose seemed to throb. As usual, I couldn't look away from the explosion of dark holes that dug deep in his face; as a child, Joe had suffered from smallpox.

"Okay," I said finally and closed my eyes. The next I knew his hand was in my hair, giving my scalp a vigorous rub.

"I can feel my luck changing," Joe sang out, raising his voice for the benefit of those watching. "Anybody selling lottery tickets? Somebody hand me a racing form."

From the jukebox, Johnnie Ray belted the first lines from "Cry."

Eventually Joe stopped rubbing and I opened my eyes. Joe's face, at first a blur, slowly came into focus: the sunken cheeks on either side of the nose that carried a bluish hue and belonged on the face of somebody larger, the craters so deep they seemed to have shadows.

"Thank you," Joe said.

He'd been rubbing my head for as long as I could remember with no improvement in his luck. He hadn't hit any numbers to win any lotteries. At Hazel Park, he lost the trifecta far more often than he won, in fact I don't think he ever won. His wife had died two years before, after being run over by a streetcar. His son Archie had just been sent to Korea. Maybe this was one reason he got along well with my uncle.

"What's the matter?" Joe said. "You seem ferklempt."

I didn't know what he meant. His wife had been Jewish, from Lithuania, and Joe sprinkled his conversations with Yiddish expressions, snatches of Polish, and sometimes Lithuanian.

"I found my uncle's drawings," I told him. "Of Wojtek."

Joe smiled. "Aren't those something? I don't know why he ever stopped."

"And you showed them to someone?"

"That's right. We both did."

"He said he didn't remember too well."

Joe's hands were on the bar and now he pushed back, away from me, and frowned. "That's probably a blessing. Are you sure you want to hear this? It's not too pretty."

I said I did, of course I did.

"Okay then." He took the dishtowel from his shoulder and wiped his face, removing the sweat that had formed there. "I guess Izzy was more nervous that day than I thought."

After glancing at my uncle at the other end of the bar, Joe told me what had happened. There'd been a meeting set up at the Polish-American Club, where Joe maintained a membership; as a bar owner, he was a respected member of the Polish community and belonged to a few clubs and associations. Once he'd seen my uncle's sketches, and recognized the appeal that the Polish Second Company's soldier bear would have among the transplanted Poles of Detroit, Joe had asked around the club to see if there were any writers, publishers, or news reporters that might be located who would take an interest in Uncle Izzy's drawings. Someone was found—Professor Casimir Sobocienski—who had once taught at the Jagiellonian University in Krakow, and now headed up the Slavic Studies department at Wayne State. A morning meeting was arranged at the club, to which the professor brought his wife, a beautiful woman according to Joe, thirty years younger than the eminent scholar. That morning, when my uncle met Joe at the bar, Joe could see Uncle Izzy was nervous, a typical artist in doubt of his talent, so Joe suggested a shot of vodka to soothe the jitters, to which my uncle readily agreed. What Joe didn't know was that Uncle Izzy had already been soothing the jitters back in his flat, quite liberally it turned out. This didn't become apparent until my uncle stumbled and nearly fell going up the stairs of the Polish-American Club, then was afflicted with a fierce case of hiccups when he sat down across from the professor and his wife.

"Chrusciki was served," Joe informed me. "And your uncle got the powdered sugar over everything. He was drinking water to get rid of the hiccups and it mixed with the powder on his lips. After a while he looked like a mad dog, foaming at the mouth."

On the walls of the Polish-American Club were large pictures of famous Polish heroes. When introductions were made, my uncle felt compelled to stand up and include the unsmiling faces looking down on them, saluting each and every one.

"Hail, Tadeusz," he said to the painting of Kosciuszko. "Where were you when the Soviets came?"

To Joseph Conrad: "Why did you change your name, Teodor?"

To Paderewski: "For a prime minister, Ignacy, you were one hell of a piano player."

To Bronko Nagurski in his muddy leather football helmet: "Rah, rah, rah. You showed America what polaks are good for: football!"

He applauded Madame Curie for being the "mother of the atom bomb." He called Pilsudski "our very own anti-Semitic dictator, not as bad as Hitler maybe, but bad!"

Then he said to Professor Sobocienski: "Where is David Ben-Gurion on this illustrious wall? Now *there's* a Polish hero."

None of this would have mattered to the professor. He was a liberal-minded man. But after finishing with the heroes on the wall, my uncle turned his attention to the professor's wife. By now Uncle Izzy had lost his capacity for glib conversation and was humiliatingly drunk. Directly outside the meeting room was the club's dance hall. Someone had been checking the sound system that morning for a dance that night, and every time a waiter entered, bringing more coffee, water, or chrusciki, bits of music could be heard: waltzes, marches, and polkas. On one such occasion, my uncle stood up and lurched across the table for the hand of the professor's wife.

"What are you doing with that stuffed shirt?" he mumbled. "Let's polka."

The professor stood then too, and accused my uncle of being drunk.

"Nazdrowie," my uncle said, raising his coffee cup in toast and spilling it over everything.

"It was mishegas," Joe said now. "A pure and utter fiasco."

He was quiet then. For the moment we stared at each other, both wondering, at least I wondered, what it was in my uncle that caused him to continually fail. I've always thought of luck as an outside force, determined by sources unpredictable and largely unknowable: destiny, grace, karma, the alignment of stars. But my uncle, I was beginning to see, seemed to conspire in his own bad luck, like a circus clown about to be kicked in the rear who bends over to present a better target. As though he knew he deserved it, and it was okay with him.

"So nothing's ever happened with those drawings," I said to Joe.

"Not a thing. And it's a crying shame."

He reached in his shirt pocket for his pack of Chesterfields. After extracting a cigarette, he drummed one end on the bar counter, tamping down the tobacco.

"So Izzy's taking you to Cleveland," he said, lighting the cigarette. Smoke drifted from the corners of his mouth, recalling the hookah-smoking caterpillar from

"Alice in Wonderland," a movie my uncle had recently taken me to see despite my protests I was too old to see it.

"I lost money on that," Joe told me. "I bet that Ilona would never let you go." He made a clicking sound with the inside of his cheek.

"I'm sorry," I said.

"Sorry?" Joe squinted at me through the cigarette smoke. "Don't be sorry, kid. You're going to Cleveland."

But I *was* sorry. I couldn't help it. While Joe, like my uncle, was one of those people who never seemed to get a break, unlike my uncle, he did nothing to encourage misfortune. No one was more deserving of a little luck.

"I mean about losing the money," I said.

"Oh, it's no big deal." He waved his hand in the air, dispersing the veil of smoke that was forming between us. "It's what I'm good at. My special talent."

Looking down the bar, he watched Uncle Izzy place his hand on Florin's back, in the middle of some longwinded story.

"I just wish I felt better about his chances for success." Joe shook his head and again made the clicking sound. "That woman doesn't care if he lives or dies."

The jukebox music had ended by now. The only sound was the drone of the Tiger announcers chronicling another defeat, the whir of the fan blades, and the mirth in my uncle's voice as it escalated in volume; he must have been nearing the end of his story.

What woman? I wondered.

I watched Joe suck in more smoke from his cigarette. He was leaning over the bar again, looking down at my uncle, and I could smell the tang of his Wildroot hair oil. Suddenly he started coughing, something he did like nobody else. Whether due to his chronic smoking or the mustard gas he'd inhaled during World War I, his lungs were never mucus free. You noticed it when he spoke, clinging to his sentences that were always accompanied by a subtle wheeze; and when he coughed, you could hear it whipping around inside, smacking against his lungs, the thick ropes of it. There was nothing to do but look away; the coughing could take a while. When he finished, his face was as red as the cherries that went in his drinks. Taking the dirty towel from his shoulder, he would then mop his face and gasp for the breath that had been eluding him.

"Excuse me," he said now, once he finished gasping.

After taking another drag from his cigarette, he pointed the ash end in the direction of my uncle. "You know, some people think your uncle puts bullshit in paper bags and sells it." Squinting, he looked at me through the curtain of new smoke, confidential-like. "I'm not one of them. I believe the guy. I just question his judgment sometimes. Like chasing this skirt after all these years."

"What skirt, Joe?"

His eyes grew wary. Pushing back from the bar, he said, "What has Izzy told you about the trip to Cleveland?"

"He said he's going to look for a job. That we're going to visit my Great Uncle Jakub."

Joe nodded. "All right then. If that's what he said, then that's why you're going."

He noticed my bag of potato chips. It was lying unopened on the bar and pushed it toward me. "Eat your chips. You haven't touched them."

I ripped open the bag, selected a large chip, popped it in my mouth.

"This woman I mentioned," Joe said, "she's probably a very minor part of your trip. Inconsequential."

I ate another chip.

Joe lowered his voice. "I'd appreciate it if you didn't mention this to Izzy—that I told you about a woman."

"Okay, Joe," I said, in between potato chips.

"And especially don't mention it to your mother."

Leaning toward me, Joe nodded his head, raising his eyebrows.

I nodded mine.

The day I thought would never come finally came. My mother drove us to the Greyhound station on Washington Boulevard and Grand River. She parked her prewar Packard across the street and took us into the Cunningham's drug store for lunch. There was still an hour before departure.

"Be sure these aren't damaged, Izydor," she said, sliding the tin box containing Great Uncle Jakub's chrusciki along the lunch counter.

"Don't worry, Ilona. Not a speck of sugar will be lost from these angel wings."

All morning she'd been frying the delicate pastries and sprinkling them with powdered sugar. My uncle and I had sampled our share, to the point where I'd nearly lost my appetite for lunch, but how could anyone resist a Cunningham's grilled cheese sandwich, chased down with a chocolate malt?

"I hope you're as careful with Chester," my mother said.

"Like I said, Ilona, don't worry."

When lunch was over, after again making me promise that I'd phone and send postcards, my mother gave me a quick kiss on the cheek, turned, and walked swiftly from the bus depot. She was not one for big public displays of emotion.

Since we still had fifteen minutes, my uncle bought a cigar and we strolled around the station lobby as he smoked it, reading all the advertisements for the fine places you could go on a Greyhound: Miami, the Grand Canyon, Hollywood; there was no poster for Cleveland.

Minutes before departure we boarded our bus—a Silversides Supercoach built by GM. It had blue trim accenting a freshly washed steel body that gleamed invitingly in the afternoon sun. On each side was a sleek white greyhound, caught in full running stride, that didn't look like it would ever be caught. We claimed two seats a few rows behind the driver, who hadn't boarded yet. I took the window. The seats were adjustable and well cushioned, more comfortable than anything we had at home.

At exactly our departure time, a man in a silver-gray uniform climbed up the steps and took account of us passengers. Slowly, he walked down the aisle, smiling at everyone, saying things like: "Hello there." "Welcome aboard." "Hope you enjoy the trip."

When he reached me, he said, "This your first time on a big dog, young fella?"

I looked at my uncle. "He means a Greyhound," my uncle said.

I nodded at the man, the driver as it turned out.

"Well, here you go then." He handed me a silver pin in the shape of a greyhound, just like the ones on the sides of the bus.

"Put it on," my uncle said.

I pinned the shiny, fleet-looking dog to my shirt pocket.

"There you go," the driver said. "Thank you for traveling with America's favorite bus company."

The trip itself wasn't particularly eventful. After stopping in Rockwood, then Monroe, then over the border in Toledo, we lost sight of Lake Erie entirely until we drew closer Cleveland. What we did see of the lake wasn't all that attractive. There were no log cabins as I had been picturing, no fishermen in canoes hooking rock bass and lake perch, no teenage girls lying on towels in the sand or waterskiing in skimpy swimsuits. The portion of the lake we saw was somber and austere, dotted with barges and tugboats and damaged-looking freighters, black-hulled or rust-colored, that poked along sluggishly close to the shore. Instead of cabins and cottages there were warehouses, factories, and processing plants, red lights flashing high upon smokestacks that smeared the blue sky with lead-colored smoke. The air had a reek of sulfur and iron that penetrated even through the closed bus windows.

After Toledo we hit farm country. The land acquired

a slight roll, the acres of corn, fruit, and cow pasture gradually rising to form knolls where every so often stood a house, barn, and silo. We passed fruit stands and roadside diners with gas pumps off to one side. There were warning signs for leaping deer but never any leaping deer. At one point, we rounded a sweeping bend and drove past a freshly tilled field.

"What's that smell?"

"Fertilizer," my uncle said. "To make corn grow as high as an elephant's eye."

"It smells like—"

"It is," my uncle interrupted. "That's what it is."

I was shocked. Growing up in the city, I'd never considered the nature of fertilizer. It seemed wrong that something we ate, in this case corn, was dependent on something so rank and vile for its growth. The odor was worse than the Dodge plant. Fortunately, we soon left it in our wake. After a while, the lazy repetition of fields, orchards, and farmhouses grew monotonous.

"Where do we stop next?"

"In Berlin Heights, about an hour from here. We should be in Cleveland before nightfall."

I was getting sleepy. I'd eaten all that food.

"Tell me a Wojtek story."

More and more I had to ask my uncle for these. Since our time on the roof, he'd grown stingy with his Wojtek stories, sharing the bear's exploits only if he was certain he had a willing listener. I'd hurt him; that much I knew. But I had no idea how to repair the damage. In the first place, it was uncomfortable even bringing up the subject, and when I did he only made a joke or changed the topic—something I became proficient at as I grew older.

"I love you," I said.

Prior to my announcement, my uncle had been gazing out the window at a meadow of white-faced cows. But he looked at me, then. It had been at least a year since I'd said I loved him. I think I said it that afternoon for the same reason I always did: I needed to know I was loved in return.

"Of course you're aware," my uncle said, "that Wojtek took some journeys too. Like the one on the troop ship with us from Egypt to Italy. He never rode on a bus though. You have him beat there, Czeslaw."

"Tell me about the troop ship."

"You've heard that story a thousand times."

"I like hearing it."

My uncle looked at me. He was an intelligent man. He must have understood by then why I was so attached to the story: it was the last time my father was to play a part in any of Wojtek's adventures. Following the movement of troops across the Mediterranean came the Battle of Monte Cassino, where Wojtek would gain most of his fame by helping the men load artillery shells during the relentless fighting, and my father would lose his life. On the troop ship though, all of that lay in the future as the men enjoyed a brief respite from the war, the last good time my father was to have.

"Okay then," my uncle said. "Since you've heard this before, you know that going to sea was new for Wojtek. Because the ship was so jammed full of soldiers, he had to stay on deck, lashed to the mast by a long chain. Sometimes he would climb the mast for exercise, going as high as the chain allowed."

I closed my eyes and imagined Wojtek scaling the ship's mast, peering across the limitless sea. It must have seemed quite strange after the desert and mountains of the Middle East.

"It was the first time Wojtek was among a large group of soldiers, other than us polaks in the Second Transport Company. He was as intrigued with them as they were with him. But what he liked best were the seagulls."

Wojtek would stand on his hind legs, Uncle Izzy explained, and try to grab the birds with his paws, never with any success; the only thing he ever caught was the curiosity of his new shipmates. Seeing how gentle he was with the Polish soldiers, the new men wanted to befriend Wojtek too. With that aim, one day two soldiers from another unit approached Wojtek and offered him chocolate. Wojtek took it, of course, and while he munched the candy bar, he allowed one of the soldiers to rub the fur on top of his head. "Why don't you just kiss the hairy brute?" my father yelled from among the crowd that had gathered. My father! I imagined his face as he delivered his immortal line; it would have worn a smirk, like the one my uncle utilized, but friendlier, less dour.

Not thinking my father's suggestion a wise course of action, the two men began to back away from Wojtek when suddenly the bear's paw shot out and grabbed one of them by the leg, knocking him to the deck. Spurred on by the hoots of laughter this generated from his audience, Wojtek began to play with his captive, rolling him from side to side, licking his face. Just as the terrified soldier was about to crawl away, Wojtek caught him by the ankle and stood up, turning the man upside down, emptying his pockets of their contents: spare change, a Zippo lighter, a rosary, a pack of cigarettes, fingernail clippers, a comb, a pair of dice; it all came clattering onto the deck. Then Wojtek pulled the man's pants down—or up rather, since the man was inverted.

"Of course this drew the most applause of all," my uncle said. "Piotr and your father finally made him let the man go. But it took awhile. Wojtek was having too much fun."

"Did he get in trouble?"

"No. Everyone knew it was just good fun. He was seasick after that. He sat on the deck, holding his head in his paws, moaning like a merchant seaman with a five-alarm hangover."

"Did everyone laugh?"

"No. Everyone else was seasick too."

By then it was late afternoon, the sun behind us, stretching the shadows of billboards, trees, and telephone polls. My uncle sat quietly, watching the scenery unroll, each new vista nearly indistinguishable from the one immediately prior.

"After that came the Battle of Monte Cassino," Uncle Izzy said quietly.

Of course I knew all about Monte Cassino. I'd heard about it often enough. By the time my father and my uncle's company arrived there, three previous battles had been waged, but the mountains had remained in the hands of the Nazis. Finally, after a brutal seven-day battle, the Polish Second Army, under the direction of General Wladyslaw Anders, and including Lance Corporal

Izydor Wierzbicki but no longer including Lance Corporal Aleksy Wierzbicki, managed the task. Wojtek had helped by loading and unloading ammunition during the weeklong siege, hefting heavy boxes of twenty-five pound artillery shells from the backs of lorries. Everyone was amazed by Wojtek's work ethic. One of the men was moved to create a drawing showing Wojtek carrying a large shell, set against the background of a steering wheel. This icon became the badge of the entire company, appearing on caps, the lapels of uniforms, the sides of vehicles and other equipment. I myself was the possessor of such a badge, a gift from my uncle that now lay at the bottom of my sock drawer back in Detroit. I'd never worn it to school, afraid it might be taken from me, or worse, that it would require me to explain the story behind it, which was the story of Wojtek. I wasn't up to the task. I didn't want people looking at me the way they looked at my uncle as he related Wojtek's escapades. I felt odd enough already in the company of my peers, most of whom had the full allotment of parents, and whose mothers spent their days cooking up recipes for dinner, not for pharmaceuticals.

"Look, Czeslaw."

My uncle pointed out the window. A blue convertible was passing on our left, a Cadillac, in the lane normally reserved for oncoming traffic. The young driver kept his eyes on the road, but the passenger in back, a man in a white suit, white shirt, and a black string tie, was waving at us with his cowboy hat, shouting something I couldn't hear. In his other hand, the man held a whiskey bottle, which he now brought to his lips, taking a swallow. The man whooped then, a sort of high-pitched yodel or rebel yell I could barely hear through the window; then the car's rear whitewalls flashed past and it swerved back into the eastbound land, inches in front of the bus, seconds before another car whooshed by going the opposite way, horn blaring.

"Crazy idiot," my uncle said.

I looked at him as he stared out the window. Something had felt peculiar when he spoke those words and I realized now what it was: my uncle was the one calling somebody crazy, so often it was the other way around.

In Berlin Heights there was a twenty-minute stopover. When we stepped off the bus to see what we could see, it turned out to be not very much. While I used the rest room in the Post House restaurant, my uncle visited the store on the corner, the only establishment that seemed to be open on this forlorn looking backstreet a few blocks from the sleepy main drag. By the time I took my seat on the bus again, my uncle hadn't returned, so I used the opportunity to examine the book he was reading: *Nightfall* by David Goodis. It seemed to be about an artist who couldn't remember things. Other than that, I didn't learn much, except that the artist knew some good-looking women, judging by the blonde on the dog-eared cover. Once we were on the road again, my uncle reached in his paper bag and pulled out a bag of potato chips and a bottle of Faygo red pop, then passed them both to me.

"Just like Joe Dzirada's," he said.

For the next few miles I contentedly munched my chips and sipped my soda, noticing lights pop on in the farmhouses we passed, interrupting the dusk with buttery glow. After a while, my uncle reached into his bag again. This time he pulled out something stronger than red pop.

"Don't tell your mother," he said, unscrewing the cap from a pint of Samovar vodka. "It pains me to drink this fake-Russian crap. But it was all they had."

After a lengthy swallow—the pint was a third gone—he said: "A man needs to be allowed certain things in life that permit him to loosen the grip of the world." He was looking out the window as he said it, as if speaking his truth to the encroaching dark, the disappearing trees. "A man is imprisoned. A man loses the love of his life. A man goes to war. A man loses his brother. A man is due at least some recompense for these tribulations." He turned to me. "Wouldn't you say so, my young friend?"

I couldn't answer. For the past month I'd been hoping, then believing, that this new sober version of my uncle was going to stick around. Joe Dzirada's mention of the mysterious woman my uncle was apparently going to see in Cleveland was the first warning that all may not be as it appeared. I had ignored it. Couldn't my uncle meet someone from his past and still find plenty of time to look for a job? Still make good on his promise not to drink? Now though, I knew that nothing had really changed at all. My uncle had probably been drinking right along, although in lesser amounts, and hiding it quite successfully from my mother and me. I felt like I'd been sucker punched in the gut by Jozef.

"A man deserves to feel good now and then." He elbowed me in the shoulder. "Right Czeslaw?"

"I guess so."

"Guess? What's to guess?"

Apparently my uncle wanted more from me; I was unwilling to provide it. He made himself feel better with another drink.

"Don't drink too much," I said. "The woman you're going to see won't like it."

Immediately he lowered the bottle of Samovar. Slowly, he twisted the metal cap back on and placed the pint back in his sack.

"Who told you? Joe Dzirada?"

"He didn't mean to."

My uncle sighed. By now it was dark. For a while I watched the road posts fly by, each one bright white, lit by the headlamps of the bus.

"Her name is Katarzyna. We were going to be married."

When I looked at him, a faint smile creased the corner of his lip. "Then the Russians kissed up to the Nazis and I went to the gulag." He shrugged. "We lost touch."

After a moment he looked at me and seemed to brighten. "Then recently, completely by chance, Czeslaw. It was fate. I swear it—"

Looking back out the window, he shook his head, apparently unable to account for this atypical stroke of good luck.

"—My friend Bronislaw saw her on a streetcar. He thought it was Katarzyna but he wasn't sure, so he rode the same streetcar again and she was on it again. Then he rode it many times until he worked up the nerve to say: 'Are you Katarzyna Zawadzki from Zielonki?' 'I used to be,' she answered. 'I'm Katarzyna Nowak now.' She'd moved to Cleveland to be with her husband, who'd found work at Universal Steel. But her husband had died. After expressing his condolences and waiting a proper number of streetcar rides before troubling her further, Bronislaw asked, 'Well, Katarzyna, how would you like to meet your old sweetheart, Izydor Wierzbicki?'"

My uncle was beaming now.

"What did she say?" I asked.

"She said that she wouldn't."

"Then why are you seeing her?"

Apparently, being turned down by his old girlfriend was a cause for celebration; my uncle was still smiling.

"Because, Czeslaw, women often do not know what they really want. Men are no better. I am a prime example. But don't be fooled by appearances. People say no because that's the first thing their minds tell them." He tapped the side of his forehead with his index finger. "It's the easiest answer. Often it makes logical sense. But—" Now he raised the same index finger. "—Once they give the matter further thought—when they consider it with their heart, their soul, and their intuition—they sometimes reach a different conclusion."

"They conclude yes?"

"Yes. Sometimes they just need a little push to move from the initial *no* to the deeper, more heartfelt *yes*."

"And that's why we're going to Cleveland?"

My uncle nodded. "When she gets a load of me, in the flesh, she won't be able to help herself. At least I hope not."

Although I had my doubts, I kept them to myself. My uncle may have guessed them, however, because he felt compelled to add, "We were deeply in love, Czeslaw."

Outside the bus window there were more lights now, signs for motels and restaurants. We passed an intersection with two gleaming gas stations, where uniformed attendants filled the tanks of Fords and Plymouths, squeegeed bugs from windshields.

"You lied to us," I said. "You said you were going to Cleveland to look for a job."

"And I will look for a job—once Katarzyna accepts my proposal."

In the window glass I could see our reflections, pale and insubstantial, like two wandering spirits floating among the streetlights and neon. If what my uncle was talking about actually happened, I might soon be uncle-less, in a sense, as well as fatherless. I wasn't sure I was ready.

"Of course you were right about watching my drinking," my uncle said. "That's why I cut back in the first place—to present myself in the best possible light."

He winked at me, then, something he did all the time when he was drinking, but had managed to avoid the whole previous month.

The Hennepin was a seaman's hotel near the shore of Lake Erie. The lobby carpet featured a pattern of whaling ships, high waves, and whales, but the sun pouring in the front windows day after day had turned the waves powder blue and the ships and whales a common gray. On top of the carpet, against the beige stucco walls, sat leather chairs with curved metal frames, the leather cracked in places, showing its age, as did the inhabitants of the chairs—old sailors and I'm sure a few landlubbers—some of them missing teeth or other more alarming features: eyes, fingers, parts of their legs. There were photos of ships on the walls, mostly Great Lakes freighters. Potted palms added a tropical touch. When you entered from the street and made your way to the front desk, you immediately noticed the smells: tobacco smoke, a whiff of old plaster from the flaking walls, muscle ointment, coffee grounds, refuse, and whatever the residents upstairs had been cooking on their hotplates.

We were staying there because Bronislaw had no room at his house—he had a wife and four kids—and it would be too much of an imposition on Great Uncle Jakub and Great Aunt Roza. Also, Uncle Izzy knew the owner of the hotel, a man named Danek. After the war, they'd both been merchant seamen. Danek had placed a cot in our tiny room, perpendicular to the Murphy bed that, when not in use, folded up into the closet. Sleeping on the cot that night, I felt strange and adrift, noting occasional voices in the hall, the traffic in the street, and the caws of seagulls. It was my first night away from home and I wondered if I hadn't made a mistake. Upon our arrival, Danek had pulled out a bottle from behind the front desk and he and my uncle toasted each other until it was gone. Now my uncle lay snoring in the creaky bed, sometimes moaning unintelligibly in Polish. In the light from the streetlamp outside our window, the dresser loomed ominously, as if foreshadowing the bleakness that awaited me in the not-so-distant future: a shabby hotel room like this one, a dresser scarred by cigarette burns with drawers that wouldn't open. I could almost hear my mother: "Is that what you want, Chester, to end up like your uncle? It's what will happen if you don't do your homework." I'll study, Mama. I won't tune in *The Green Hornet* until every page is read and every assignment completed. I was surprised how much I missed her.

The following morning, though, in the light of day, with birds chirping and flapping their wings furiously every so often as they landed on our window ledge, the room didn't seem so horrible. On the wall was a picture of Jesus touching his sacred heart. In the dark he had looked like a bearded fanatic. On the chair next to my uncle's bed was a stack of folded towels, on the dresser a bowl of oranges.

My uncle, of course, was still asleep, so after I got up and used the bathroom down the hall, I dressed and went down to the lobby. Behind the desk, in almost the same position I'd left him the night before, was our host Danek. He was talking to a man wearing a steel nose shield.

"Good morning, Czeslaw," Danek called, rather gaily for someone who'd consumed the amount of alcohol he had. "Where's your uncle, still in slumberland?"

I said that he was.

"This is Vilmos," he informed me, slanting his eyes at the man with the curious nose ornament. I couldn't take my eyes off it.

"Vilmos, this is Czeslaw, nephew of my old shipmate."

"Pleased to meet you," Vilmos said, then lifted his

nose shield as if tipping his hat. Underneath, his nose stopped about halfway down; dangling from it were strands of cartilage.

"This is what happens," he said, "when you put your nose where it doesn't belong."

He replaced the nose shield and smiled.

"Don't listen to him," Danek said. "He ran into some shrapnel during the war."

"I was sniffing around a French whore," Vilmos said. "But I had no money. Her pimp didn't like that." He smiled again, revealing two gold teeth.

I looked away. My eyes landed on the glass case beneath the front desk counter and its assortment of cigarettes, cigars, pipe tobacco, matches, candy bars, licorice, gum, and postcards.

"I'd like some postcards," I said.

They were laid out along the bottom shelf: buildings and beach scenes, crowds at Municipal Stadium, museums, streetcars, all the attractions of Cleveland.

"Which ones?" Danek asked.

"One of each."

He gathered them up—there were twelve in all—and slipped them in a slim brown bag. I watched him as he did it, his green eyes and red hair that turned sandy on his arms, over his sunburned skin. I didn't want to see Vilmos.

"No charge," Danek said.

"I wish that was the case with the French whore," Vilmos added. When I inadvertently looked up, he winked; I wondered if he might be drunk.

Turning away, I noticed a bookcase on the far side of

the lobby, about as far away as I could get from Vilmos. After thanking Danek for the postcards, I walked over to investigate. There were mysteries mostly, with a few adventure yarns and stories about the sea. Something called *Death Ship* caught my eye and I spent the next hour leafing through it, keeping one eye on Vilmos to make sure he didn't decide to leave the front desk and come take the seat next to mine. If he threatened to make the slightest move in that direction, I was ready to bolt out the door and take a sightseeing tour of the neighborhood, although judging from the glimpse I'd had last night, there wasn't much to see.

At about ten o'clock, the bell over the front door tinkled and in walked Bronislaw.

"Czeslaw, where's your Uncle Izydor?"

"Upstairs," I told him. "Probably still asleep."

"We must wake him. We are due at Jakub and Roza's."

But my uncle was already awake. As we approached our room, we heard him whistling, something he rarely did. When we opened the door, we found him rubbing hair tonic into his scalp, smiling into the cloudy mirror. A cigarette burned on the dresser, which he picked up and stuck between his lips.

"Good morning," he said, the cigarette bobbing with each syllable. "The saints are smiling. It's a glorious day."

Replacing the cigarette in a burn mark on the dresser, he reached for his comb and began stroking his hair in place. With his left hand he patted it flat.

"The saints will be free with their blessings today," he said. "Grand things will happen."

When he was ready, we tromped down the stairs on

our way to Bronislaw's Oldsmobile. Hearing the racket of our footsteps, we stepped even more forcefully, creating more noise—three healthy males on their way to take care of the day's business. In the company of Bronislaw and my uncle, leaving the hotel that morning, it was the first time I felt like a man.

"Here's to love," Danek called out as we passed the front desk. He held up a shot glass filled with amber liquid. Vilmos did the same.

When we stepped outside, I saw my uncle was right; it was a glorious day. The sun was warm on my skin, but a breeze from the lake made the tree leaves swish, creating a fluttery pattern of shadow and light on Bronislaw's blue Oldsmobile. Once we climbed inside, Bronislaw started right up and pulled away from the curb with a chirp. Driving with one hand, he let the other arm dangle out the window, his fingers on a cigarette. Our route took us east and south, away from the water, until the streets became leafier the nearer we came to Warszawa, the section where Great Uncle Jakub and Great Aunt Roza had their home.

"What do you suppose happened to that guy's nose?" my uncle asked.

Bronislaw glanced at him. "The guy at the desk? I was talking to him last night after I dropped you off. He said his wife bit it off in a fight."

"Jezus Christus."

"You can say that again."

Bronislaw turned left off a main avenue, then right on a residential street lined with small brick and aluminum-sided homes. At the corner he parked the Oldsmobile under an elm tree, in front of the only two-story house on the block. The house was skinny in front but looked like it went pretty far back. Constructed of red brick, it had flowerbeds under the windows, and a small cement porch on which two people sat in lawn chairs. When she saw us, the woman stood up and waved. The old man didn't move.

"Hello, Roza!" Bronislaw shouted as we climbed from the car. "Look who I brought."

The woman continued waving. Uncle Izzy waved back. I waved too.

"You remember Czeslaw," Bronislaw said as we approached the front porch.

"Oh, Czeslaw," she said in a high-pitched voice, fluttery with emotion. She hadn't seen me since before I could remember, since before she'd decided traveling didn't agree with her and she'd be happier staying in Cleveland. From that time on, Great Uncle Jakub had been traveling alone.

"Come here," she said, her thin arms extended.

Even on a warm day like this one she was wearing a sweater. I stepped into her trembling embrace.

"Dobry chlopak," she said, patting my back. "Dobry chlopak." After a moment, she released me.

"This is Izydor," Bronislaw said, "Aleksy's brother. You knew him in Zielonki."

"Oh, Izydor," she said, her arms again reaching out. Now there were tears in her eyes.

My uncle went to her and they hugged, said things in Polish, the words thick and sibilant and beyond my comprehension. When they were done, there was nothing else to do but look at Great Uncle Jakub. Except in a very general sense, he seemed not to recognize we were there. His gray eyes were fixed on a spot somewhere beyond us, out near the street, and his lips moved without making sounds, as if he were having the dream where you try to articulate some great peril, but have lost your ability to speak. Saliva had collected at the corners of his mouth. Great Aunt Roza took a handkerchief from her sweater pocket and wiped it from his lips.

"It's all right, Jakub," she said, patting the bony knee beneath the bulky gray slacks. He'd lost a lot of weight. I remembered a more vigorous great uncle who hoisted me up to the ceiling to see how much I'd grown, and entertained my mother with stories of the old country while he sat at the kitchen table, skinning apples with her potato peeler and eating them, their green and red husks curling over the red and white tablecloth.

"He had a stroke," Great Aunt Roza informed us. "They say the next one could kill him."

We all looked at him in light of this information, then glanced away, as if gazing too long might cause the same misfortune to happen to us—as if strokes were somehow contagious.

Once we'd helped him inside—Bronislaw at one elbow, my uncle at the other, Great Uncle Jakub taking tiny bird steps so the whole process seemed to take a long time—we ate. Great Aunt Roza had prepared pierogi stuffed with cottage cheese, over which we ladled warm Log Cabin syrup. There were also scrambled eggs with the bacon cooked right in, and of course Mama's box of chrusciki. For a while all was silent as everyone ate, the only sound coming from Great Uncle Jakub, who at one point passed gas, apparently without noticing.

When Uncle Izzy finished eating, he pushed back from the table. "Wyborny," he said. "Thank you, Roza. All this good food reminds me of my old friend Wojtek."

Bronislaw shot me a glance. There was egg in his moustache. Was he familiar with Wojtek too?

After setting her cup back in its saucer, my great aunt smiled at my uncle. "I don't remember Wojtek," she said. "Is he from Zielonki too?"

"No. I met him in Persia," Uncle Izzy said, looking at me then glancing away.

"Is he a good friend?" Aunt Roza asked in her singsong voice.

"Practically my only friend. Except for Czeslaw."

Bronislaw audibly cleared his throat.

"Oh, and Bronislaw," Uncle Izzy added. "I can't forget my good friend Bronislaw."

Following lunch, my uncle and Bronislaw drove away in Bronislaw's car. The plan was for me to spend the afternoon with my great aunt and great uncle, then join Bronislaw and Uncle Izzy for dinner. After Great Aunt Roza and I helped Great Uncle Jakub into the living room and lowered him into an overstuffed armchair where he promptly fell asleep, Roza pulled out a small suitcase from under the sofa and began sharing its contents with me: photographs, many from Poland, some capturing my mother, my dad, and my uncle when they were roughly my age. In one, my father wore a light-colored suit with a flower in the lapel.

"That's Aleksy at his confirmation," Roza told me.

Another picture showed a circle of girls in white dresses, each with a hand on one of the long, streaming ribbons drooping down from a tall pole they all surrounded, a maypole Great Aunt Roza informed me. "Your mother is second from the right. The pretty one."

The photographs occupied us through the early afternoon. Great Uncle Jakub's cadenced snores broke like waves over Roza's small, fragile voice as she described the participants in the photos and the significance of each occasion. After a while, we left Jakub to his dreams and she took me out to see her garden, which was so much like my mother's I thought Mama must have taken pictures. There was even a white trellis at the back of the yard, leading to the alley. Roza unspooled a rubber hose and watered her flowerbeds until the soil turned black and peaty and smelled like wet coal. Then she enlisted my help in eliminating the few weeds that had taken root.

"Don't yank," she instructed. "Pull slowly so you get the whole weed."

"I know. My mother showed me."

Roza stood up and looked at me, one hand on the small of her back, the other clutching the wilting corpses of weeds. "Your mother is a sweet woman," she said. "She does not let her suffering consume her." She shook her weeds at me. "Don't forget to call her, Czeslaw."

"I won't."

"Good boy. Dobry chlopak."

"Why do you say my mother's sweet?"

Something about Great Aunt Roza—perhaps the fact she was old and therefore non-threatening, and seemed to enjoy my company—inspired my confidence.

Now, like an Indian scout, she lifted her hand above her eyes to provide shade from the sun—the better to see me.

"You don't think your mother is sweet? Your mother adores you, Czeslaw."

"Oh, I know that," I said, although I didn't really, and *adores* seemed a bit overstated for the feeling I imagined my mother held for me. "It's just that she doesn't always do things that—well—"

Roza lowered her hand from her forehead. "I see."

"You haven't been with her in a while."

There were hollyhocks nearby and they'd attracted some admiring bees, which seemed to divert my great aunt's attention.

"She hasn't had it easy," Great Aunt Roza said. "Rubbing up against the roughness of the world can cause a person to grow a thick skin." She looked at me then. "Do you think I'm sweet, Czeslaw?"

I did in fact; it seemed the perfect word to describe her. I nodded my head vigorously.

She sighed. "I used to be terribly hard to get along with. I wouldn't go anywhere, you know. If someone wanted to see Roza, they had to come to my house and steel themselves against my bitter glare." She laughed, just once. "Not many people did."

"Why were you bitter?"

"We lost our son. Like you lost your father." Shaking her head, she started walking toward the house. "I felt like God had turned His back on me—on Poland—on whatever goodness was in the world."

Next to the back door stood a dented trash can. She lifted the lid and deposited the weeds inside, then waited for me to do the same.

"Here I was, safe in America, the Nazis defeated, the Soviets an ocean away, and I was still hating, hating, hating," she said.

I dropped the weeds in the can. She clamped the lid down.

"It just got to be too much after a while. Being miserable is hard work."

She opened the back door and we climbed the few steps that led to her kitchen. From a cupboard she pulled two glasses, then opened the refrigerator and filled them both with lemonade.

"Do you know what finally happened?" she asked. "I realized something—that if I hated God, and that if God had made me in His likeness like it says in the catechism, then I hated myself." She placed the glass in front of me on the kitchen table. "That's the religious view," she told me, smiling again. "And I really did hate myself. But what I didn't realize until that moment was that I was punishing myself. God didn't love me any more or less than any other human being in the world. He wasn't making me miserable; I was. So I stopped."

I took a sip of lemonade. It was tart, sweet, frosty cold. From the other room, Great Uncle Jakub let loose a loud snore, informing everyone within earshot he was still alive.

"Why did you hate yourself?"

"I think because—" She looked up at the ceiling. "—I was giving myself too much credit. When life didn't turn out the way I hoped, I blamed myself, not just God. I felt I'd failed somehow, when actually there was very little I could have done. Except change my attitude."

Great Aunt Roza smiled. "That happened six years ago," she warbled. "I just wish it had been sooner so I could have been a better wife to that sweet man sleeping in the other room." She sipped her lemonade and fixed me with a level stare. "Go call your mother," she said.

I did as she suggested. The phone was in the hallway next to the living room, sitting in a little nook carved into the rose-colored wall. My mother answered on the second ring.

"Hi, Mom."

"Chester! Are you okay?"

"I'm fine. I'm calling because I said I would."

"Are you at Jakub and Roza's?"

"Uh-huh."

"How was the bus ride?"

"It was good." I told her about the farms, the cows, the rolling green fields.

"What about the hotel? It's a dump, isn't it?"

"No. It's okay. There are clean towels and sheets." I didn't mention that I was sleeping on a cot. "I bought postcards at the front desk."

"Is your uncle there?"

"He's out looking for a job."

"He's not drinking, is he?"

"No," I answered after the slightest hesitation, praying she wouldn't notice. My rationalization was that he wasn't drinking that very minute; at least I didn't think he was.

"That's good," she said. "Do you love me, Czeslaw?"

"Uh-huh."

"I love you too. I miss you. You've never been away

before."

"I'll be home soon."

"Eleven more days. That's an eternity."

For a moment there was silence. Not even Great Uncle Jakub disturbed it from his armchair in the other room. It crossed my mind that he might be dead. When my mother asked to speak to Jakub, I said he was asleep, would Great Aunt Roza do? Fine, my mother said, so I went and fetched Roza from the kitchen, then walked into the living room and strategically positioned myself on the sofa near the hall, believing from there I could listen to their phone conversation. I hadn't foreseen they'd be speaking in Polish. With my plan thwarted, I turned my attention to Great Uncle Jakub, who was still in the armchair, head flung back against the rear cushion, face tilted toward the ceiling. Inside his open mouth, the dentures had separated slightly from the upper gum; and from the corner of his lip, a rope of drool stuck to his stubbly skin that had taken on a grayish pallor, the same color as the boiled liver my mother forced me to eat when I was anemic. His hands clutched the arms of his chair as if he were bracing himself against some disaster—a hurricane or earthquake. But everything was very still. And I wondered again if he wasn't dead.

"Great Uncle Jakub?"

He didn't move. In the hallway, my mother said something funny and Great Aunt Roza laughed.

"Great Uncle Jakub?"

I stood up and moved closer to Great Uncle Jakub. From this distance, I could smell the menthol rub he used and the mothballs his clothes had been stored in.

His lips were purple. From his nostrils protruded a tangle of hair and a single pearl of snot, but it didn't move; there was no breath to move it.

"No!" I cried as the enormity of the situation hit me.

My cry didn't go unheeded. Great Uncle Jakub opened his eyes.

At first he blinked for a while, opening and closing his mouth like a turtle, as though he really had been brought back from the dead and was having trouble readjusting. But of course that wasn't the case. My great uncle had merely been sleeping the deep, almost comatose sleep of old people who have suffered strokes. My shout had awakened him. Only now, unlike earlier, he seemed able to recognize that people were around him, even if he didn't know who they were. When he saw my face, he shot forward in the chair and started yelling in Polish.

Almost immediately Great Aunt Roza came hurrying in, also speaking Polish. She pressed Jakub's head against her stomach and began slowly rocking him, her words becoming softer and more soothing the longer she rocked.

"You gave him a fright," she told me. "He was afraid that he'd died and you were our son, that they'd been reunited in heaven."

"I'm sorry."

"It's not your fault, chlopak."

Later, after taking my great uncle upstairs, Great Aunt Roza went into the kitchen to start making dinner. Because I still felt bad about the scare I'd given my great uncle, I stayed in the living room, alone with my feelings, leafing through the pages of the three magazines that weren't printed in Polish: *Life, Look,* and *The Saturday Evening Post.* At five o'clock I fully expected Uncle Izzy and Bronislaw to walk in the door and take me to dinner. But that didn't happen. At six o'clock Great Aunt Roza poked her head in the room.

"Would you like some chicken soup?"

"No, thank you. I'll wait for my uncle."

"Don't feel bad. Jakub gets easily disoriented. Half the time he thinks I'm his mother."

She went back in the kitchen. A half-hour later, bored with the magazines, I was standing at the window identifying the makes of the cars driving by, when Bronislaw's Oldsmobile pulled up at the curb. But only Bronislaw got out and walked toward the front door; there was no sign of my uncle.

"He's still out looking for work," Bronislaw informed me. "I'll take you to dinner. We'll catch up with him later."

After thanking Great Aunt Roza for her kind hospitality, as my mother had specifically instructed, Bronislaw and I drove off into the deepening evening.

"Where did my uncle go job hunting?"

Bronislaw glanced at me for a moment and sighed. After taking a drag of his cigarette, he flipped it out the window.

"Let's eat," he said. "Do you like kielbasa?"

We stopped at a diner called Stan's. They served kielbasa in buns, topped with cheese and kapusta; back then nobody did that.

"Your uncle didn't have much luck today," Bronislaw said. We had both finished our kielbasas. I was thinking of ordering another.

"He didn't find a job?"

"He didn't look for a job." Bronislaw looked at me and frowned. "He went to see his old girlfriend, Katarzyna. You've heard of Katarzyna?"

I nodded, waiting for him to go on. But first he lit a cigarette, blowing the smoke at some donuts displayed on a tray beneath a plastic lid.

"Well, it didn't go so well," he said. "I guess you could say she rejected him."

I felt my skin prickle with indignation. "Where is he now?"

He took another puff of his cigarette and this time sent the smoke to the ceiling. "That's the problem. Nobody knows."

"We have to find him."

"I've been looking, Czeslaw. When I went to pick him up, Katarzyna told me what happened. He'd been gone for hours. I've called the hotel numerous times but he hasn't returned. I've been to the bars near the hotel, the bars near Katarzyna's—"

He closed his mouth, raised his eyelids, shook his head. "Nothing," he said.

"Call again. Call the hotel."

"In a while, Czeslaw. Have a golumpki. I tried again just before I picked you up."

"Can I try?"

"You think that will change anything?"

He sighed, reached in his pocket, dropped a nickel in my palm, then a matchbook with the hotel name and phone number. I found the phone in the back of the diner, next to the men's room.

"Hennepin Hotel," a voice answered after the seventh ring.

"Is Izydor Wierzbicki in? He's in room seventeen."

"Um, just a minute."

The voice didn't sound like Danek. It was more nasal and whiney—Vilmos.

After a period of time longer than a minute, another voice came on the line.

"Hello, Czeslaw?" Danek.

"Yes?"

"Your uncle's here. He came back. My God, he gave us a fright."

"Is he all right?"

Silence.

"Danek?"

"He's here, Czeslaw. That's all I can say. Come have a look."

For the better part of two days my uncle stayed in his room, confined to his bed, in his own way dealing—or not dealing—with his failure to win Katarzyna. I learned later it was because she was engaged to another man— her first husband had been dead three years—and not because she was cruel and dispassionate, as I'd imagined her to be.

My uncle was devastated. He'd expected great things, seeing in Katarzyna's reemergence a sign that, at last, his fortunes might be taking a turn for the better. Fate was finally on his side. In the weeks before meeting her, he'd imagined a string of overdue blessings playing out in his life, starting with Katarzyna agreeing to be his wife, and including a move to Cleveland where he would land a well-paying union job, then find a nice house with a yard for the three kids and the dog they were going to have. All this he told me later. At that moment, in that now grim hotel room, he was barely able to speak. From what he'd told Danek when the cab driver brought him back to the hotel, I learned that Uncle Izzy had started drinking after leaving Katarzyna's, that later he'd been involved in a bar fight and dumped on the sidewalk, where a compassionate cab driver had found him and loaded him into his cab, then driven him to the Hennepin. The driver, a fellow veteran, would accept no payment from Danek.

At first Uncle Izzy just laid in bed sleeping. He had a black eye, a swollen nose, and a purple bruise that colored one side of his face. His lips were puffed up and a jagged cut climbed from the corner of his mouth to below his right temple. He'd thrown up at some point; the room still smelled like puke, although Danek or someone had wiped away any further evidence.

"Not his shining hour," Danek said.

Bronislaw and I had just taken our first look at my slumbering uncle. We were all squeezed into the tiny hotel room.

"He looks like he was run over by a truck," Bronislaw said.

"A vodka truck," Danek added, slanting his green eyes in my direction. "Remember what I told you, Czeslaw."

Earlier, at the front desk, he'd entrusted me with a

fifth of Smirnoff and the instructions to feed my uncle a shot glass full whenever he woke up. Now Bronislaw pointed at the bottle.

"Do you really think that's a good idea?" he said. "Giving him more siwucha?"

"Believe me, I know alcoholics," Danek said. "Which is a club Izydor Wierzbicki belongs to. If his alcohol intake is cut off entirely, considering the amount his body is used to having, well we could have one hell of a problem." Danek glanced at me. "You wouldn't want to witness such a problem."

"The heebie-jeebies?" Bronislaw inquired.

Danek nodded, then Bronislaw nodded slowly too.

"What are the heebie-jeebies?"

"Alcohol withdrawal," Danek explained. "The DTs. A person's body doesn't know what to do without the alcohol it's used to getting. It can go a little crazy."

"He could get the shakes," Bronislaw added.

"Or worse," said Danek. "He could hallucinate rats or snakes coming through holes in the walls, or feel like insects and worms are crawling all over his body. He might cry out in terror because to him they're very real."

I shuddered at the thought of rats. The previous winter I'd seen them in the cellar near the furnace, where they went to get warm. I could imagine their tiny feet padding up my back and into my hair, the swishing of their long, pink tails.

"He could even have a seizure and die," Danek said.

Not that! Oh, God. I would watch my uncle like a cat watches a morsel of tuna. If he fluttered an eyelash, I would be ready with the vodka.

Once Danek and Bronislaw left, I pulled the straight-backed chair over close to my uncle's bed. When he didn't move a muscle for over twenty minutes, I thought it might be safe to open the book I'd brought along, *Death Ship*. After every half-page I stopped and observed my uncle. For the most part he just slept. When he moved, it was to find a more comfortable sleeping position. Occasionally he murmured unintelligible things, sometimes twisting his head from side to side on the pillow. Once he started thrashing under the covers, moaning what sounded like: "No, no, wooaaugghh." I unscrewed the cap from the vodka bottle.

"Uncle Izzy, it's not real. Do you want a drink?"

He didn't hear me, just kept twitching around like a hooked perch in the bottom of a rowboat. Finally he stopped and the next minute he was snoring. At three in the morning, Danek, who'd checked in many times, told me to get ready for bed.

"Vilmos will take over," he said. "He can never sleep anyway."

When I returned from brushing my teeth, Danek was still there, still waiting for Vilmos.

"You know," Danek said, "I think another trip might be good for your uncle. A longer trip this time." He eyed me significantly. "I think he should go see Wojtek."

"In Edinburgh?"

"Where else?"

The thought of it made my heartbeat accelerate until I felt it pounding between my ears. Despite all my uncle's allusions, and my mother recently saying we might go when I entered high school, I had never thought that visiting Wojtek was anything remotely possible. To my mind, Edinburgh had always been a storybook place, as fantastical and inaccessible as Oz.

"Did you know I met Wojtek?" Danek asked.

I shook my head. Speech at that moment eluded me.

"On the ship to Italy, the M.S. Batory. I was in a different company than your uncle but on the same boat. You could see how much those men loved that bear." Danek's eyes seemed to see beyond the present, as if they were looking back to the blue Mediterranean and the Batory's voyage. "And the bear loved them," Danek said. "Especially Piotr, the Lance Corporal who had charge of him. And your uncle, of course."

"Wojtek loved my uncle?"

"Yes, I think so. It was quite apparent."

"What about my father?"

Danek turned to look at me. Slowly, he shook his head. "I'm sorry about what happened to him," he said. "But I never knew your father. I didn't become friends with your uncle until later in Scotland, after the war." He smiled then. "Don't look so glum. I'm sure Wojtek liked your father too. But it's only natural that the bear would have a special place for Piotr and your uncle. They bought him from the Persian boy."

"I thought my father did."

Danek's eyelids lowered and he started to frown. "That's not what Izzy told me."

We both looked at my sleeping uncle. He'd managed to yank the covers up almost over his head, so only his hair was visible, no longer brown as it had been in Great Aunt Roza's pictures; now it was streaked liberally with gray.

"Izzy was different then," Danek said. "So were we all. But your uncle—"

He glanced out the window at the darkness beyond.

"Your uncle has just never been able to get back on his feet. It was okay when we were seamen after the war, moving from port to port. But when he got back on dry land and moved to Detroit, he seemed to lose interest. It was like the life started seeping slowly out of him—from some old wound, like air leaking from a tire. Anyway—"

Again Danek stared out the window. I could see his reflection in the box of darkness, his red hair turned muddy gray, like a criminal from Planet Krypton banished to the Phantom Zone.

"I think seeing Wojtek might do your uncle some good," Danek said. "It might be good for the poor bear too, caged up in that zoo."

"I think it's a great idea," I said. "And I can keep an eye on him just like tonight, to make sure he doesn't drink too much, or have seizures."

Danek turned slowly and gave me a look. "You're not going anywhere except back to Detroit. School starts next month."

"Not for three weeks."

"That's not enough time. You have to find a ship. Then there's the crossing itself. It might take that long to get there."

"But he needs looking after."

"Perhaps so." Danek looked at my uncle, who had started snoring again. "But not by you. Christ, your mother would kill both of us if she heard us talking now."

"Do you know my mother?"

Danek squinted at me. "I've heard your uncle talk."

"She's not as bad as he says. Actually she's very sweet. You can ask Great Aunt Roza."

Opening his mouth, Danek stopped and seemed to reconsider. In the ensuing silence, in the spaces between my uncle's snoring, we heard the footsteps of Vilmos as he made his way down the hall. Danek pointed at my cot.

"Sleep tight," he said. "Don't let the bedbugs bite."

"There won't be any bedbugs. I'm sleeping on a cot."

"Good then. You don't have to worry."

Once he was well enough to sit up in bed, eat solid food, and think as clearly as he was ever capable thinking, my uncle was able to see the wisdom of a trip to visit Wojtek. Especially after Danek offered to lend him some of the money. But in response to my impassioned pleas to be taken along, he had only one answer.

"No."

"But you'll need someone to talk to—about Katarzyna and how she hurt you."

"No."

"I'll only miss a little school. I can make it up next summer."

"No."

"But Mama said I could go when I got in high school. That's not very far away."

"No."

"But it was my father's big wish."

"No."

For the entire next day this went on. I kept bringing up my father even though I wasn't sure now if it had truly been his wish that my mother and I meet Wojtek, just as I was no longer certain who had accompanied Piotr when he purchased the bear cub. Had my uncle lied to me or to Danek? Either scenario seemed possible. Uncle Izzy may have lied to me to try to elevate my father in my eyes, though my father scarcely needed it; conceivably my uncle felt a responsibility to keep my father's memory large and untarnished, as a standard for me to aspire to, the preferred alternative to the dubious example my uncle had been presenting. Or he may have simply lied to Danek, pretending he'd played a bigger role in Wojtek's evolution to build himself up in Danek's eyes—one of the usual reasons people lie. Whatever the case, it didn't diminish my desire to meet the soldier bear. Whether it was my father's wish that this should happen, or my uncle's wish that I believe it was my father's wish, it didn't change the fact it was my wish. And I'd been wishing it ever since my uncle appeared on our doorstep three years prior and started telling me about my father and Wojtek.

Toward the end of the day, my uncle rose from his bed and cleaned himself up. Even after a shower and shave, he looked like he'd been in the ring with Rocky Marciano. Later that evening, Danek took us to dinner down the block at a place called Lucy's. It was Monday and they were having a fish fry: walleye, steelhead, and white perch yanked straight from Lake Erie by Lucy's husband and his fishing buddies.

There it was decided that Danek would drive us to the Greyhound station the following morning, where my uncle would buy a ticket to Hoboken, and a return ticket for me to Detroit. I was crushed. My twelve-day visit to Cleveland was being reduced to four. Worse, my uncle was going to see Wojtek and leaving me behind. Still, I hadn't mentioned a word of this to my mother in our phone call that afternoon; partly because I didn't want her to know my uncle had gotten drunk, and that his real reason for the Cleveland trip had been to see a woman, not to look for a job; and partly because I was eleven years old, an age when hope is as abundant as popcorn. I still believed I stood a chance of accompanying my uncle, and I was determined to keep that hope glimmering, like a bright little diamond, until I was finally forced to board that Detroit bus.

Over the course of dinner, the details of my uncle's voyage were discussed. In Hoboken there lived a man named Konrad, a ship captain who operated a small tramp steamer between the East Coast and Europe. Danek and my uncle had crewed for Konrad when they were merchant seamen, forming a bond—a rare thing between captain and lowly crewmembers—in the waterfront dives of Hoboken. Earlier in the day Danek had called Konrad to see if my uncle might sail with him to Edinburgh. It turned out Konrad had just returned from Oslo and wouldn't be returning to Europe until October; however, he checked around and found that another captain, a man named Lothar, would be sailing to Liverpool in four days aboard a freighter called The Blackhawk. Because Lothar and Konrad were friends, and Lothar had a cabin available, my uncle was able to book passage at a good rate.

"When was the last time you were on a ship?" Danek asked my uncle. We had finished eating and they both lit thin cigars: Phillies Cheroots.

"With you, you son of a bitch. When we delivered those rivets to Algeria."

"I wonder how many of those rivets ended up in the hides of French Legionnaires." Danek smiled at me.

My uncle took a puff of his cigar and let smoke drift from his lips.

"There's nothing like the sea," Danek said, "to escape the disappointment encountered on dry land."

My uncle looked down at the table and sighed, taking note, it appeared, of the remains left on his plate: a nest of uneaten coleslaw, a dollop of tartar sauce partially obscuring a trio of soggy fries, a lemon rind squeezed dry of its juice.

"Well, Czeslaw," Danek said, "what do you think? Can we get your sad sack uncle to tell us a story about the illustrious soldier bear?"

"That would be nice. Since I won't be able to *see* Wojtek in person."

Ignoring my complaint, my uncle said: "Czeslaw's heard every Wojtek story there is. Many times over."

"*I* haven't," Danek objected.

"Get Czeslaw to tell you. He knows them better than I do."

Uncle Izzy then extinguished his cigar in the puddle of tartar sauce on his plate, producing a sweet, unpleasant smell. Glancing at me, Danek rolled his eyes.

"All right," I said. "I'll tell a Wojtek story."

I chose the tale of Wojtek and the soldiers from India, which happened after my father was killed during the Battle of Monte Cassino. Once the battle was over, Wojtek was given his own sleeping quarters: a huge timber crate turned on its side. But at night in that foreign land, he often grew lonely and would crawl into one of the nearby tents to sleep with Piotr or one of the other men. My uncle said Wojtek was lonely for my father; that he hoped to find him in one of those tents but never did. One night, however, when my uncle's company was camped next to a unit of Indian infantrymen, one of those Indian soldiers received the surprise of his life. He awoke to find himself looking at the muzzle of a four-hundred pound bear, who was fast asleep with one paw laying on the soldier's hip, perhaps in a gesture of friendly familiarity, at least from the bear's point of view. Of course the soldier screamed for his life, awakening Wojtek and everyone else. When the soldiers of my uncle's company ran to see what the trouble was, they found Wojtek encircled by a group of Indian soldiers in their nightclothes, each with a rifle aimed at the bear. "Don't shoot!" the Polish soldiers cried. "He's tame. He's one of us." After a tense minute the Indian soldiers lowered their guns.

I told the story in a straightforward manner, not bothering to mimic an Indian accent, as my uncle did when he told the story, not employing any of his theatrics: the raised eyebrows, prolonged pauses, squinting looks of incomprehension. Still, I had my listeners' attention. Watching me closely throughout, my uncle kept a wry smile on his lips as the story unfolded. When I finished, he clapped his hands.

"Bravo, Czeslaw," he said. "Very well done. Didn't I tell you, Danek? What do you need me for?"

As he watched me, though, my uncle's smile slowly faded, replaced by a look of curiosity. "One question, Czeslaw. Why that story?"

I couldn't answer him then. "I don't know," I said, and my uncle let it go at that. But later that night, lying on my cot, the reason came to me. It was because at the moment he was surrounded by those Indian soldiers, Wojtek nearly died. It wasn't on the front lines during the Battle of Monte Cassino, but in the friendly confines of his own camp, where the odds against death were much higher than on the front lines, which hadn't saved my father, after all, from the shell that claimed his life. If Wojtek had died at that moment, it would have seemed completely real to me, with a strong sense of irony, the way life, in my small sampling, was proving to be.

By the time we reached the bus station the next morning, I had pretty much accepted the fact I would be arriving in Detroit that evening the same way I left it: aboard a Greyhound. While waiting for my uncle to return with the tickets, I'd even visited the newsstand where a man with one arm gave me change for my dollar bill so I could call my mother. I was only waiting until I knew the exact time I'd be arriving. After getting change, I'd taken a seat on a bench next to a woman working crossword puzzles. Across the room I noticed Uncle Izzy standing at the food counter. After placing some coins on the counter, the waitress slid him a cup of coffee, which Uncle Izzy then took to the newsstand, where he scanned the front page of a newspaper, and then purchased what looked like a map.

"What's a five-letter word for *scoundrel*?" the woman next to me asked.

She was thin and wore round-framed glasses. Her hair was pulled back in a bun. Behind her lenses, her blue eyes squinted for the answer.

"Snake?"

"Ah!" Her eyes widened. "Thank you." She lowered her pencil; then stopped. "It won't work. It begins with a *K*."

"There you are, Chester," my uncle said.

We both looked up as he sipped his coffee, then wiped his lip with his thumb. His face was still puffy and bruised. The woman must have noticed. I was just grateful he hadn't called me Czeslaw.

"Am I interrupting something?" he asked.

"Oh no," the woman said. "I was just asking your son if he knew a five-letter for *scoundrel*, beginning with *K*."

My uncle thought for a moment. "Knave?" he said.

"That's it! Perfect. Thank you." Leaning over her book, the woman entered the letters in boxes.

"Here's your ticket."

I took the rectangle of paper from my uncle, avoiding his eyes, and especially not wanting to look at the ticket and see the word *Detroit*.

"Thank you," I said, as he swept old newspapers off

the bench so he could sit down next to me.

I had picked out a man in a suit who was walking by and I followed him until he left the terminal. My uncle was studying me, I could feel his eyes, but I couldn't return his look. Who knew how long he would be in Edinburgh? What if he chose to stay there? It might be years before he saw his "son." I took a deep breath and tried to swallow the peach pit that had lodged in my throat. I didn't want to cry. I never cried.

Finally, I glanced at the ticket.

"This ticket says Youngstown, Ohio."

He narrowed his eyes and gave me a puzzled look, then pulled out his own ticket and looked at it.

"That's funny. So does this one."

It took us two days to get to Hoboken.

On the bus to Youngstown, my uncle explained why it wasn't until that morning that I learned he wasn't the only Wierzbicki who would be going to see Wojtek.

"I just wasn't sure, Czeslaw. Until I went to the ticket window."

"That you wanted to take me?"

"I wanted to take you all right." He paused, glanced out the window, then looked at me and frowned. "It's like this, Czeslaw. When your mother finds out I've taken you to Scotland, I will cease to exist in her life. She'll throw out my belongings. I'll be unwelcome under her roof. When she thinks of me, it will be with less esteem than for the dog shit she steps in and has to scrape from her shoe."

This seemed a bit overstated. My mother was actually very sweet I wanted to tell him. But as I thought about it, and how my mother had reacted to some of his escapades in the past, and how she was likely to react now to him taking me across the ocean without her permission, or even her knowledge, I could see how he might arrive at the conclusion he did. For the first time I began worrying about my own complicity in what we were doing, and to fear my mother's response to being led down the garden path by her own son. Before we'd left Cleveland, my uncle had made it clear to me that despite saying she might let him take us to see Wojtek, she'd had in my mind some future date when I was in high school, not the present moment with school fast approaching, when we were supposedly only going to Cleveland. We needed to be very careful with her, my uncle said. At his suggestion, I'd even called her before boarding the bus and said I'd be spending the afternoon fishing on Lake Erie, while Uncle Izzy was searching for a job. And I'd dropped a postcard in the mail—Bob Feller in his windup with his left foot high in the air—saying I hoped to get to an Indians game soon, and that I loved her and missed her very much.

"The fewer people who know about this, the better," my uncle said. "I don't want Ilona blaming Bronislaw and Danek the way she's going to blame me."

"And me," I said.

"No, not you, Czeslaw. Your mother loves you more than anything in the world. Don't you know that?"

"I guess so. Everyone keeps saying so."

"She'll be hurt, but she'll forgive you. She understands how much seeing that bear means to you."

"But why won't she forgive you? Seeing Wojtek means a lot to you too."

"I'm not eleven years old." He looked out the window. Eastern Ohio was passing us by. "I should behave more like an adult. Have a steady job. Not be chasing after a bear. Sometimes I think I'm chasing the past. That would make me a fool, Czeslaw. Do you know why?"

"Because you can't catch it?"

My uncle nodded and looked at me briefly; then back out the bus window. For the rest of the trip to Youngstown he was silent, almost despondent. Once we reached that city, the plan was for us to forgo bus travel and rely on our thumbs to attract us rides. We wanted to save money for our time in Great Britain; it was unclear what awaited us there. My uncle had only put us on the bus to Youngstown because he didn't want to be seen hitchhiking by Danek or Bronislaw or Vilmos, remote though that possibility was. In Youngstown we found a market where my uncle bought some provisions, then a Rexall drugstore where he purchased a marking pen. Behind the drugstore was a dumpster filled with cardboard boxes. My uncle ripped one apart and printed *Hoboken*, in large block letters, on the largest piece. Then we followed the directions we'd been given out to the major east-west highway. It was after seven p.m. by then and the sun was dipping down in the west, resembling a red Necco Wafer, which reminded me of a story Sister Rosemarian liked to tell. It involved a young girl who had recently received her first Holy Communion, but then began wondering if the round wafer she swallowed at Mass was truly the body and blood of Jesus Christ. Even in light of God's miracle-working power, it didn't seem possible. Then one Sunday she decided to try a test. During Communion, she secretly spit the white wafer into her handkerchief and took it home. After locking herself in the bathroom, she unwrapped the white host and stuck it repeatedly with one of her mother's hatpins. After a moment, to her shock and amazement, the host started bleeding. The girl screamed and fainted. When they heard her scream, her parents had to break down the bathroom door to see what was the matter. They found the girl sprawled on the floor next to the host, which was oozing blood. Everyone was pretty shaken up by the incident. The girl had to spend time in a mental ward and later ended up becoming a nun—a nun who eventually shared her story with Sister Rosemarian. My problem with the story was that it seemed a little too convenient to the purposes of Sister Rosemarian to actually be true. As we stood there on the edge of the highway watching the sun fade and the landscape turn to silhouette—and since nobody showed the slightest interest in picking us up—I decided to try the story on Uncle Izzy.

"What happened to the host?" he said when I finished.

"What do you mean?"

"The wafer, the host. It's supposedly the body and blood of Christ, right, after being miraculously changed during the Eucharist?"

"Uh-huh."

"Well that's a pretty important thing, a piece of God

Himself you might say, sitting on the bathroom floor, bleeding. What happened to it? Your story makes no mention."

The highway was quiet, no cars to be seen in either direction. Nearby stood an oak tree, its trunk coated with road dust, snatches of birdsong coming from its higher branches.

"I don't know," I said. Now I was intrigued. What *would* you do with the host? You couldn't very well flush the body and blood of Jesus Christ down the toilet. That would be sacrilege, wouldn't it? But if not that, what? Should you call an ambulance to try and stop the bleeding? Or a priest? And how long would a host bleed? For a few minutes? For eternity?

"That's why the story's baloney," my uncle said. "If it was true, you'd know what happened to the host."

"Maybe it's not important to the message," I said.

"The story is nonsense," my uncle replied. "It's hokum the nuns made up to keep you kids in line."

I'd figured as much; even nuns, the brides of Christ, lied when it suited their purposes. My uncle handed me the *Hoboken* sign.

"Here, you hold this," he said. "Maybe it'll change our luck."

He stuck his thumb out. I held up the sign. A Plymouth blew by us, raising dust. This was to be the way of it for the next half-hour as vehicle after vehicle ignored our plight, with their lights on now, until finally one stopped: a truck, a big long-distance hauler, that whined to a halt about forty yards past where we stood. Gathering our bags, we ran to catch our ride.

"Welcome aboard," the driver said when my uncle yanked open the passenger door. "Might be a little cramped with your bags."

"Thanks," my uncle said. "We'll manage."

He wedged our belongings between the floor and our feet, so my knees were level with my chest. After my uncle slammed the door, the driver shifted into gear, slowly released the clutch until the truck crept back onto the pavement, and drove off into the Pennsylvania night. His name was Hoagland, he said, but his friends called him Buddy. In the back he carried a load of Elmira stoves that he was taking to Philadelphia, where they would be unloaded and he would pick up some Philco televisions. His truck was a Mack; it said so on the steering wheel, where there was silver emblem of a bulldog. I imagined the envy in Jozef's eyes when I told him I'd been a passenger in a Mack truck.

"Hey, Buddy," my uncle said. "Care for a snort?" He was holding a pint of vodka. I don't know where it came from.

"Well now. Don't mind if I do. Just a little one."

When Buddy was done, my uncle took the bottle and treated himself to a lengthy swallow, then put the bottle in a grocery bag.

"Beautiful night," he said.

"They're all beautiful," Buddy replied. After a moment, he went on: "I mean when you're out on the road, the miles flying by, your window open a crack to let in the aroma of the night, what's not to like?"

"You're not a married man then," my uncle said.

"Oh, I am, I am." Buddy smiled at my uncle then

looked back at the road. "I'm as married as a man can be."

"You don't miss her at all?"

"That's my problem. I *keep* missing her. She keeps jumping out of the way when I try to run over her with this truck here."

Buddy chuckled to himself. He had wavy blonde hair, which he ran his hand through now. His eyes were inky blue.

"I'm just kidding," he said. "I love my wife. If anything happened to her, I mean if she were to die, I'd drive this truck off a cliff so I could go join her."

"But that would be suicide, Buddy. According to the Catholic Church, you'd go to hell for that. I don't think you'd find your wife there, at least not from what you've said about her."

Buddy glanced at me, then at my uncle, and then he turned back to the road. After that, not much more was said. West of Snow Shoe, Buddy pulled over and let us off. He was taking the road to Philadelphia while we continued on toward the Poconos. It was nearly midnight by then. The headlights of eastbound vehicles were infrequent. Crickets chirped so loudly that if they'd been part of a radio broadcast, I would have turned it down. Some source of water was nearby; I could smell mud and a hint of sewage. Up above, the sky was crowded—with planets and thousands of stars.

"Look. The Big Dipper."

My uncle glanced in the direction my finger pointed. "The Starry Plough," he said. "We'll be in Great Britain soon."

He reached in the grocery bag. Out came the vodka

bottle.

"Why do you do that?" I asked.

The bottle hadn't reached his lips. It wavered in the air.

"Why do I drink?"

"Not just drink. Everyone drinks."

"Well it must be okay then."

"But you end up sick in bed. You get in fights."

The bottle continued its journey and my uncle drank down vodka. When he finished, he wiped his lips on his sleeve.

"I'm like Buddy," he said. "He doesn't want to live without his wife. I don't want to live without this."

Holding the bottle up in the moonlight, he jiggled it. We both watched the contents slosh around.

"In sickness and in health," he said quietly. "It's my medicine. Sometimes I overdo it."

"Danek says you're an alcoholic."

My uncle thought about that. "Maybe yes," he said. "Maybe no. Anyway, there are worse things."

"Like what?"

"Like not knowing what you are. In that case you don't know what makes happy. You chase after the wrong things thinking they're the right things."

By now headlights were approaching. He placed the bottle back in the bag and stuck out his thumb. I picked up my sign as a car sped by, then swerved to the shoulder, scattering gravel and raising a froth of dust, tinted red by the glow of the car's brake lights. From the passenger's window an arm reached out and beckoned us to join it.

"Let's go," my uncle said. "Before they change their

mind."

The car was a Cadillac, a '46 or '47. Gashes were gouged in the passenger side as if it had scraped against a guardrail or another vehicle. Inside sat a man and a woman, both of them black. They were young and dressed for a date it looked like. My uncle started opening the door behind the driver, who was the woman.

"Whoa, whoa, whoa," said the man, whose arm had summoned us. "There's a condition to this ride." He turned to look at my uncle with eyes that were bloodshot, unfocused, and seemed to roll in their sockets. "The condition is you drive."

"No problem," my uncle said without hesitation, a statement that wasn't exactly true. Because although my uncle did sometimes drive on rare occasions, he didn't do it well. And he didn't have a license.

"Let's see your license," the loose-eyed man said.

My uncle reached for his wallet and showed the man his identification card, which had his picture, name, and address, but clearly was no driver's license. The man squinted his eyes at the card. He wore a white shirt, partially untucked; his tie and suit coat lay slumped on the seat.

"Okay," the man said. "Dorena, you are officially relieved of your driving duties."

"Hee-hee-hee," Dorena said, leaning forward and banging her head on the steering wheel. She groped for her things on the seat around her: her silver purse, a pack of Beeman's gum, the fur stole that went with her lime green dress. "Good thing you two haints appeared like that out of nowhere. He's too juiced to drive this boat."

"And she's too high on candy." The man pushed open the passenger door with his foot, stood up, and did a clumsy dance before opening the backdoor and collapsing in the backseat.

As the woman performed her own version of the dance on the driver's side, my uncle said: "I know about Cadillacs. I worked in a car factory in Detroit. You have nothing to worry about."

"Worry?" the man said. "We don't believe in it. Do we, sugar?"

"No way," Dorena answered. Still outside the car, she reached behind her with one hand and located the backseat, then lowered herself carefully down. "Worry's for people who have something to lose," she said, sliding across the seat to get close to the man, resting her head on his chest when he raised his arm.

"You can drive now," the man said. "Home, Jeeves."

"Yes, sir."

We piled our luggage between us on the expansive front seat and hopped in. After studying the instrument panel, my uncle turned the key in the ignition, stepped on the gas, and the car took off—in reverse.

"I'm sorry," the woman said when he stopped. "I was gonna back up for y'all, but when I turned my head I got the spins."

"No problem," my uncle told her.

"It's an automatic," the man said. "Just put it in drive and goose it."

"Of course."

This time my uncle managed to urge the car forward, but with such suddenness that the rear wheels spun holes in the roadside dirt until the Cadillac fishtailed onto the highway.

"Easy, cowboy," the woman murmured from the backseat.

Once on the pavement, my uncle hunched over the steering wheel and stared out the windshield, keeping the Cadillac at a manageable forty miles per hour even though the speed limit was fifty-five. Our passengers took no notice.

"Where are you two headed?" my uncle asked, speaking over his shoulder into the backseat.

"Huh? What?" the man muttered.

"Where are you traveling to?"

"Brooklyn," the woman said. "The Park Slope section."

"We're going to Hoboken," my uncle said brightly.

"That's good. We can drive from there," the woman replied.

My uncle continued peering out the window, his hands tight on the wheel. After a while, he relaxed and began driving faster—forty-five when I glanced at the speedometer. He started whistling—some polka song.

"What are you whistling?" the woman asked. The man was snoring now—loudly.

"Oh, nothing. Some song I can't remember the name of."

"We're musicians. Sonny plays piano. I sing."

"You're kidding."

"That's right. We're actually bible salesmen."

My uncle tried to look at her in the rearview mirror; he wasn't sure what to make of her.

"No, we're really musicians," she said. "Although I did

used to sing in a church."

"How did you become a musician?" my uncle asked, a thoughtful expression on his face, as if what the woman said didn't sound too hard, he might become a musician too.

"Stupidity," she said. "Muleheadedness."

I glanced at my uncle, who looked briefly at me. In the backseat the woman yawned extravagantly.

"I guess it takes a little talent," she went on. "I'm glad that's all it takes because that's all I got. I'm not the only one who knows it." After a moment, she said: "Sonny's different though. He's going to make his mark. Sonny Clark. Remember that name. You heard it here first."

"What type of music?" my uncle asked.

"Jazz. Bebop."

"Like Benny Goodman?"

"Different." She yawned again. Her dress rustled as she adjusted her position. "Good night, Mister Chauffeur Man," she murmured. "It's sleepy-time time."

"Sweet dreams," my uncle said.

"You too, sweet manchild."

My uncle looked at me. He raised his eyebrows.

"Good night," I said, perhaps a bit too loudly.

That was the last we heard from her. My uncle kept driving and I leaned my head back so I could look out the side window at the surrounding dark—empty and everywhere, it seemed to have brought everyone in the car closer together, like little kids hiding in a closet who eventually share their secrets. After a while I fell asleep; but before I drifted off I heard the crinkle of paper, followed by the clank of a bottle knocking against something hard—a steering wheel or gearshift.

In Hoboken the next morning, before our passengers were awake, we were able to drive straight to the water and locate the bar where we were to meet Captain Konrad and Captain Lothar later that day. After turning the car around, my uncle pointed it in the direction of the highway to Brooklyn and parked it at the curb. We removed our belongings. Then my uncle stuck his head in the open curbside window.

"Hey," he said. "Wake up." He reached in and shook Sonny by the shoulder until Sonny's eyes popped opened.

"Where the fuck is this?" Sonny said.

"Hoboken. Not far from Brooklyn."

"New *Jersey?*"

He looked at the buildings on the block, the people passing on the sidewalk, the cars, the street signs, as if they might be from another country.

"Dorena," he said, grabbing her shoulder and shaking, "we're in New *Jersey.*"

"I know, I know," she said, opening her eyes, swatting at Sonny's hand. "I told the man it's okay. We're close, sugar."

We stood on the sidewalk while they wiped the sleep from their eyes and made themselves presentable. It was Dorena who sat behind the wheel.

"I know this area," she said. "Sonny's from California."

My uncle invited them to breakfast but Dorena

declined. "Not our kind of neighborhood," she explained.

After they drove off, we had most of the day to kill. For a while we wandered the town—my uncle bought a map—until we ended up in Elysian Park, where I was thrilled to find a plaque identifying it as the birthplace of baseball. Under the shade of a chestnut tree, I wrote a postcard to my mother. I knew the postmark would read *Hoboken*, not *Cleveland*, but I was hoping she wouldn't notice. It seemed better than to stop all contact.

"You need to call her too," Uncle Izzy said.

I told him I couldn't. The thought of speaking lies to her, even over the phone, made me feel like a pit had opened in the bottom of my stomach and I was falling through it, down to some dark place where I would no longer resemble the child I'd been. If this was what growing up required, I wasn't sure I wanted to.

We were sitting on a park bench, each having eaten a hero sandwich, although he'd saved some of his for the pigeons and seagulls.

"Here's what will happen if you don't call her," he said. "Tomorrow, when she doesn't hear from you, she'll be puzzled, then concerned, then, after a few hours, worried sick."

He scattered breadcrumbs and bits of lunchmeat over the sunny concrete. A cluster of pigeons started gobbling it up; there seemed to be no pecking order.

"Then she'll call her Aunt Roza," he went on, "who will check with Bronislaw. 'That's strange,' Bronislaw will say. 'He should have been home two days ago.'"

My uncle flung more pigeon food in the air. Eager beaks darted for the morsels, grabbing one, then another, then pecking at whichever pigeon was closest, to create more space for the consumption of future morsels.

"So she'll learn the whole story, at least as much as Bronislaw knows of it." By now the pigeons had gathered up all the crumbs. They looked at my uncle expectantly, clucking and cooing. "Now she'll be terrified because you never arrived in Detroit. She'll check with the bus company and find no record of your being on the bus. No one at the Cleveland station will remember you. At that point, the police could become involved. You'll be listed as a missing person. Of course, Ilona will want to talk to me. I was the last person anybody saw you with. Already she'll have guessed the truth, that we pulled the wool over everyone's eyes so you could go to Edinburgh with me. She'll pray this is true, because any other eventuality would be too horrible to imagine. God couldn't be that cruel. Well, God *could* be that cruel, but in our case He hasn't been. At least not yet."

On the bench next to me was a lone crust of bread. I started picking at it, creating confetti. Not far away, on the other side of a well-kept lawn, water glittered. That water led to the Atlantic, and on the opposite end of all that water lay Edinburgh and Wojtek. My uncle looked in that direction, thinking.

"She'll learn our itinerary from Danek," he said. "When we arrive at the dock in Liverpool, the bobbies will be waiting."

I threw my crumbs at the pigeons, aiming for an albino in the rear. I wanted him to have first crack. But in a flurry of feathers accompanied by amplified chortling, the group quickly reconfigured around the new snack in roughly the same order they'd been in before, with the albino shoved to the back. Perhaps there was a pecking order.

"What will the bobbies do?" I asked, knowing the answer.

"Send you back to Detroit. Without seeing Wojtek. They'll be a bit tougher with me."

"Will you go to jail?" Until that moment, the thought hadn't occurred to me.

My uncle leaned back against the bench hard enough to make the wood creak. "I suppose so," he said. "At least until they're sure I didn't break any laws. I don't know the British interpretation of kidnapping."

"You're not a kidnapper. You have my consent."

"But I would have smuggled you out of the country. Without Ilona's permission. I don't know, Czeslaw. You see the problem."

He tugged at his lip. From the corner of his eye he gave me the briefest look, and I knew at that instant that he was leading me on. Yes, he might spend a few nights in jail, but he knew this had nothing to do with kidnapping. He only said it so I'd call home. I felt an immediate queasiness; I understood I was no better than anyone else in his eyes, qualifying for the same sort of treatment. Maybe this was why people shied away; they had a vague sense they were being used. Sighing, my uncle looked up at the sky. A chestnut tree spread its branches there, dappling the sunlight. My uncle pointed up.

"That tree has been there for hundreds of years, Czeslaw. It was there for the first baseball game."

"I don't want to call my mother."

"Perhaps we have made a mistake. I didn't realize how hard this would be on you." Reaching in his back pocket, he pulled out his wallet. Quietly, he counted his money. "I have enough money to buy you a bus ticket back to Detroit. I was planning to work on the ship to cover part of our ship fare, and if you return to Detroit, there will only be one ship fare."

He smiled, suddenly full of understanding for my dilemma, or so it seemed.

"What do you say, Czeslaw, do you want to go home?"

Part of me did. In that case, the hard acorn in my chest might dissolve and go away. But then I wouldn't see Wojtek. Everything was becoming so tangled and difficult; unless I was willing to hurt my mother, I couldn't go with my uncle to meet Wojtek, which I had believed was my father's great wish, and had certainly been my wish since I first heard the stories about Wojtek. But I wasn't even sure now if it *was* my father's wish— my uncle may have been enhancing—and if it was his wish, that wish had included my mother. So the proper thing seemed to be to return to Detroit and visit Wojtek later when I was in high school, along with my mother, as she had suggested. But every time I pictured myself on the bus back, something inside shouted: *No!* I felt like I'd be traveling in the wrong direction, missing an important opportunity, at least as far as having my uncle involved. In spite of the fact he was still drinking and still failing, he had changed a lot recently. After three years of doing practically nothing, he'd taken the trip to Cleveland—putting in considerable effort to have me come along—and now was sailing to Great Britain. He was even willing to risk his relationship with my mother, and possibly jail time, just so that I could meet Wojtek. These were bold moves for someone who spent his time in bars and on rooftops. It seemed like something had changed for him, and that if I didn't take the chance to see Wojtek with him now, I wouldn't get another.

"I want to go with you," I said.

"Your father's dearest wish."

The tears came unannounced. I hadn't planned on crying. But I could no more control them that minute than I could stop sweat from flowing on a muggy day. To my great relief, my uncle pretended like he didn't notice.

"I have a plan," he said.

My uncle always had a plan; the fact that few of them ever worked in no way diminished the care and intricacy with which they were plotted. They all *seemed* like they stood a chance. When they failed it surprised me. Some unexpected twist would send things awry, often involving drunken behavior on his part. Now he leaned forward on the bench, resting his elbows on his knees. After a moment, he turned to me.

"Here's what we'll do. You call your mother, tell her you're having a great time but you miss her like crazy. Then say a most wonderful thing happened, and you want me to be the one to tell her about it. Then hand the phone to me."

It sounded easy and required no lying on my part. "What will you say?"

His smile turned sly. His eyes, which had recently seemed full of understanding, now took on a manic glee. "I'll say I found a job at one of the mills. And that to celebrate, you and I and a friend from the hotel are going up to a rustic cabin at Geneva-on-the-Lake for some fishing, hiking, and swimming. I'll say the cabin is very remote and barebones, and we will be gone at least five days. She shouldn't expect any phone calls or postcards."

He explained that by telling my mother this we would gain time for crossing the Atlantic, before she became concerned and "unleashed the hounds." I would hopefully have a day or two with Wojtek before "the long arm of the law reached across the pond and tapped me on the shoulder."

"What do you think?" he asked.

"Will *I* go to jail?" The thought had just occurred to me, a terrifying prospect.

"Certainly not. You're a minor."

"What about juvenile detention?"

My uncle shook his head. "I'll shoulder the blame. You don't have to worry."

After a moment of reflection, I said it sounded fine. We made the call right away, while it was all clear in our minds and my uncle was still sober. Everything went well until, when he seemed to be nearing the end of the conversation, my uncle handed the phone back to me. "She wants to say goodbye," he said. The receiver was still warm from his grip, and perhaps from the hot air he'd been filling it with.

"Hi, Mom."

"Chester, be careful. Don't go with him if he gets drunk. Especially not in a boat."

"Okay."

"Vilmos will know what to do. Do you like Vilmos?"

"He's all right."

"Does he drink? Your uncle says no."

"I don't think so. I don't really know."

My mother sighed. "I should just have Izydor put you on a bus back home. I'd feel better."

For a moment I could hear the underlying hiss of the phone lines, a kind of quiet static.

"I'd really like to go, Mom. I'm eleven years old. I can write about it at school for how I spent my summer vacation."

Silence.

"I won't do anything dumb."

"Okay Chester, but promise me one thing, okay?"

"Sure."

"Promise me your uncle is telling the truth and not some crazy story he got you to go along with."

"Um—"

"Because with him you never know. But I can trust you, can't I?"

"Yes."

"Okay. Go off to your vacation cabin then."

"Okay."

"Have a great time. I love you, Chester.

"I love you, Mom."

We met the two captains at The Hawes Pipe, a bar wedged between a warehouse and a print shop, two blocks from where the Blackhawk sat at anchor. Needless to say, it was a seamen's bar and the room rumbled with the voices of sailors recounting their exploits, or, if they'd swallowed too much grog, snoring with their heads resting on the tables.

Captain Konrad was what my uncle would later call an enigma—a sailor who didn't drink. He hadn't always been that way; when my uncle and Danek had sailed with him, he was a notable hell-raiser, drinking with his men in the bars they favored, like the one we were currently in, where much leeway was given regarding behavior, with very little ever being reported to authorities or considered inappropriate. Still, Captain Konrad frequently found himself at odds with the Lykes Bothers Line, the company that employed him, concerning certain lapses. It was this recurring state of affairs, according to the captain, that led to his late-found sobriety.

"Yes," the captain answered in response to my uncle. "I do miss alcohol. But I don't miss waking up in a pool of my own wretchedness in my own brig, or in jail in Diego Garcia with a cell full of sailors I can't understand, or in a bar overlooking the harbor watching a freighter chug away and realizing it's mine."

He wore his hair longer than my mother's, and it was going gray. His face was large and friendly, with blue eyes that wrinkled at their edges when he laughed, which he did often. "Does that answer your question?" he asked.

Uncle Izzy nodded while the captain took a sip from the frothy concoction in his glass, a mixture of milk and ginger ale. "Keep 'em coming," he had instructed the bartender.

"Has that ever happened to you?" Captain Konrad

asked my uncle. "The brig? Jail?"

"Oh, sure," Uncle Izzy responded. "But not so much anymore. I can control it."

"That's good. I sure couldn't."

Both men looked at Captain Lothar, who had been silent for the most part. He had wavy black hair, a beard and a moustache, all of it peppered with gray. His dark complexion had seemed to become swarthier as he drank, as if he was getting sunburned inside that dark bar. A white scar marked his right temple, which drew enough attention that it took a minute to realize he had a glass eye. On the table in front of him sat a tumbler of scotch, his second. He'd drained the first one, seemingly in one gulp, but with a hand so shaky it spilled some of the contents over his shirt. He'd barely touched the refill.

"What are you looking at me for?" he asked.

My uncle and Captain Konrad turned away, the captain with a faint smile. When Captain Lothar reached for his drink, his hand trembled so violently that he stopped halfway and placed it back under the table, hidden from view.

"In case you're interested," he said, "the Blackhawk's anchored two blocks away. You're welcome to board tonight."

"I was hoping you'd say that," my uncle said. He raised his glass at Lothar. "Nazdrowie."

"Nazdrowie," Lothar replied.

As my uncle downed his vodka, we all watched Lothar's unsteady hand reach for his scotch glass, grab it like a slippery fish that might get away, and raise it to his lips, sloshing much of the alcohol over the table. After finishing the drink, he banged the tumbler down on the table, where it teetered momentarily, fell on its side and rolled to the floor.

"Well, gentlemen," he said, placing his captain's hat on his head, "don't be too late. We sail at oh-four-hundred."

As he stepped from the table, I heard the glass break under his foot, but he acted as if he didn't care or notice.

Aboard the Blackhawk that night, sleep didn't come easy. Even snugged up to the dock there was a roll to the water you could feel, a small hint, I couldn't help thinking, of what lie ahead. Instead of lulling me to sleep, the gentle sway of the waves produced the opposite effect. As I lay awake, accustoming my eyes to the graffiti-marred ceiling a few feet from my face—my uncle was asleep in the bottom berth—I went over what I knew to be true at that moment. I was aboard the S.S. Blackhawk—of the Isthmian Line. Its captain was Lothar, who would pilot us across the Atlantic in less than six days' time. The cargo was canned fruit and vegetables; peanut butter, molasses, and tomato paste; maple syrup; and sacks of peanuts, dried beans, and cornmeal. The second hold carried alarm clocks. We would debark in Liverpool. From there we would travel to Edinburgh to see Wojtek. At some point, probably shortly after our arrival in Edinburgh, my mother would become aware of our subterfuge and alert the authorities of our probable whereabouts. I would be taken into custody and sent back home. I would miss some weeks of school, which didn't bother me, but I did worry about how all this would affect my mother. My blatant disregard for her authority and her feelings would hurt her—the fact I could so easily lie. Never again would I be her little Czeslaw. Instead I would become some strange, half-recognized person—cunning and sly, not so easy to love. It would be a natural reaction on her part; I was already feeling that way about myself.

My uncle said she would eventually forgive me and things would be as they had been. I had my doubts. My mother's memory was long and vivid; it took detailed footnotes. I wanted to blame my uncle for coercing me to take this voyage, tempting me with tales of Wojtek, but I had no one to blame but myself. When I'd expressed my misgivings yet again to my uncle, on our walk to the ship, he said: "Relax, Czeslaw. These things you're worried about—your mother being shocked, being hurt by your behavior, looking at you in a different light—they're just part of growing up. They would happen all on their own, whether or not you went to see Wojtek. In a way it's good it's all happening now, in one big swoop, instead of being spread over the next few years, in which case you'd be a constant source of disappointment. This way it's all over and done. Look, Mama, your son is a typical human being—a liar, conniver, driven by his own selfish interests—just like you and everyone else. Blam. She'll deal with it and you'll both move on."

Did he really see the world that way? The trouble with my uncle was that he made everything sound convincing. Like a member of a debate team, he could argue one viewpoint, then make an equally strong case for the other side. You were never entirely certain where his sympathies lie. Perhaps neither was he. It wasn't a lack of conviction, more that he was too convinced about too many different and opposing things. Underlying his enthusiasms, though, there was always a trace of sadness, like the smell of burnt sulfur after the birthday candles have been extinguished, as though he realized his expectations were unrealistic, but since he knew of no other way to instill hope in his life, he would persist.

I must have laid awake for three hours listening to my uncle's measured breathing and occasionally someone passing by in the companionway outside. When the light went off outside our porthole, it was pitch-black in our cabin, and in the darkness I felt invisible, free to assume the identity of whoever I wanted until the morning light forced me to be Czeslaw again. When I did this in the privacy of my own room, I might become Robin Hood or the Lone Ranger or Hal Newhouser striking out Joe DiMaggio, Yogi Berra, and the rest of the hated Yankees. But that night aboard the Blackhawk I needed something more diverting than an ordinary human hero, someone for whom the complexities of human emotions didn't exist, possessed of more truth and innocence, incapable of hurting his mother.

So that night I became Wojtek.

The following morning I woke up late. I'd only fallen asleep a few hours earlier when I heard my uncle getting up for his *workaway*, the task he'd been assigned to reduce our ship fare. The previous evening he and Captain Lothar had decided he would assist the cook. By the time I made it to the galley my uncle was cleaning up, rattling the large pots and pans, submerging plates, cups, bowls, and utensils into tubs of steaming water. He and I were the only ones there.

"Eggs or pancakes?" he asked me.

Wojtek liked eggs, I thought. Wojtek liked pancakes. "Both," I said.

"Help yourself. They're on the counter."

I found a plate and filled it up. There were a few slices of bacon left and I ate them standing up because that's what Wojtek would do. Next to the bacon was a pot of warm syrup and I ladled it on thick; Wojtek definitely had a sweet tooth. After breakfast I found a bench on the deck and sat down; Wojtek would enjoy feeling the sun on his fur. I watched the gulls ride the wind currents as I imagined Wojtek must have watched them on the Batory as they glided between the masts, staying close in case of food opportunities but maintaining their safe distance. I'd brought along one of my uncle's books and when I grew tired of the gulls, I started reading it. When I finished two pages, I realized reading was something Wojtek wouldn't do. After that I forgot the whole silly business.

My days on board were spent largely on that deck bench. I would either read or talk to my uncle, who, apart from helping with the meals, had his days free. In the afternoons, when the sun was warmest, we tended to fall asleep leaning against the wall our bench stood next to. Listening to the waves and the thrum of the ship's engines; absorbing the sun's soothing rays, which were never too hot due to the steady sea breeze; smelling the fresh ocean air, which had been rinsed of the odors it carried on dry land, other than a faint hint of salt; it was easy to believe there were forces for good in the world, and that if we just aligned ourselves with them, everything might work out well: we'd arrive safely in Edinburgh, my uncle wouldn't be arrested, and our trip to see Wojtek would ultimately be viewed a success by everyone involved: my uncle, myself, Danek, Bronislaw, Aunt Roza, and even in time my mother, once she saw the favorable effects it would have on my uncle and me. The sea was like a balm. I can't say if my uncle shared my reverie; I like to think he did, though. Hadn't Jesus himself been lulled to sleep on a boat in the middle of the Sea of Galilee?

Sometimes I would leave the bench to walk laps around the deck, one hand on the rail, looking for whales or evidence of other fish, or for islands, icebergs, or distant ships. All I ever saw were seagulls. Then one morning, I noticed a different bird following in the Blackhawk's wake—spindly-legged, larger than any gull.

"Are those albatross?" I asked my uncle.

He put his book down and peered at the ocean stretching behind us, the blue-green sway receding until it flattened and became one with the shimmering sky.

"No," he said. "Those look like frigate birds but we're too far north. They're probably some type of pelican."

"Why do they stay so close to the ship?"

"I'm not sure," he said, lighting a cigarette. "It could be because the ship smoothes out the waves when it passes over, which would make it easier to spot fish. Those birds scoop them right out of the water." When he exhaled, the smoke shot behind us, as if yanked by some magnet. He was quiet then, watching the waves.

"Are you thinking about Wojtek?" I asked.

"Actually, I was thinking about your mother."

"I'd rather think about Wojtek."

My uncle turned to me. "Has she ever told you about her own ocean voyage?"

In fact, she hadn't. My uncle was the one who couldn't keep quiet about the events of those years; my mother barely uttered a peep.

"I didn't think so," he said. "She's not a blabbermouth like your uncle."

"What did happen?" I asked. When I asked my mother this question, she always demurred, said it did no good to discuss it.

Another trail of smoke issued from my uncle's lips. After dropping the butt on the steel deck, he ground it out with his shoe.

"Your mother did what she felt she had to," he said.

He told me then of my mother's journey to America. Before the Nazis invaded Poland in 1939, my mother was already pregnant. After my father and uncle were dragged off to the gulag by the Russians, for supposed political activities while at the university in Krakow, my mother's parents and my father's parents pooled their resources in case they needed to save my mother. She was carrying the only family heir, after all. When the Nazi invasion happened, my mother took the family money and was directed into the forests where she found others who had escaped, and a group of partisans who helped them enter Lithuania. On the way, they were often supplied with food and guns by neighboring farmers, but when they weren't, they stole what they needed. In Lithuania, there was a sympathetic Japanese diplomat who, against his country's wishes, started granting visas to every Jew he encountered that was trying escape the Nazis. My mother was lucky enough to obtain such a visa. With it, she traveled across Russia, and then to Japan, and finally, after a couple months, to America.

"But Mama isn't Jewish."

"She said that she was. Sugihara didn't ask questions."

"How come she never told me?"

"You'll have to ask her, Czeslaw. And you thought she was just a chemist."

Uncle Izzy smiled and patted my knee; I must have seemed dazed or surprised by this new information. "She did it for you," my uncle said. "And you did something for her. You may have saved her life. Because if she hadn't been pregnant with you, Czeslaw, Ilona very likely would have stayed where she was, and died in the blitzkrieg like everyone else."

After lunch the following afternoon, I fell asleep on the bench. Sounds periodically penetrated my slumbers—Captain Lothar's heavy tread as he walked the deck, the creak of the wood bench when my uncle sat down—but nothing awoke me for hours. Then my eyes popped open, perhaps in reaction to something in a dream, which upon awakening, I had immediately forgotten. I glanced at my uncle. On his knee was a pad of blank letter paper, and he was drawing, sketching in the wings of a seagull with his left hand. Next to him were sheets of paper he'd torn from the pad; the two I could see both had drawings of seagulls.

"Wojtek tried to catch seagulls," he said. "He would stand on his hind legs and use his paws. Never successfully."

I'd just heard this story recently, on the bus. "What will you do when you see him again?"

"That's a good question. I hope he remembers me."

My uncle stopped drawing. He appeared perplexed. The possibility that Wojtek wouldn't remember him had never occurred to me. But once he said it out loud, it made perfect sense; my uncle travels across the ocean to reunite with Wojtek and the bear doesn't recall who he is. It was the sort of thing that happened to Uncle Izzy.

"He'll know you," I said, not at all convinced now that this would be the case. "It just might take time. It's been a while."

"I hope so," he said. "Because if he doesn't, it will kill me."

He started sketching again, adding gray to the bird's feathers.

"But you two were such good friends."

"Not like your father and Wojtek."

Now he filled in the gull's beak, leaving it partly open.

"Danek says it was you and Piotr who first met Wojtek, not my father."

His pencil stopped, then continued working on the bird's head, shaping it.

"Danek's mistaken."

"He said you told him that."

"He made a mistake!" My uncle stopped sketching and stared at me. "It was your father, Czeslaw. Maybe I was drunk and said something stupid to Danek, or maybe he was drunk and misunderstood, but it was your father who first met Wojtek. Do you understand?"

He seemed almost desperate. I nodded my head.

"Good," he said. "Always remember that."

The next day the weather turned ugly. After breakfast, a slate gray sky descended and the sea seemed to absorb its ominous hues, then rose up in whitecaps to greet it. The ship pitched and shook as showers of wind-whipped spray leaped over the bows, darkening the deck. My uncle and I retired to our cabin where we were sick for two days, heaving up everything in our stomachs, which was often just air, into metal buckets thoughtfully provided by Captain Lothar.

On the day we arrived in Liverpool, the weather had improved, and by then, I guess, we'd acquired our sea legs, because even though the Blackhawk continued to rock and careen, the effect on our stomachs wasn't as jarring and we were able to stand on the deck and watch the waterfront take shape, ghostly and gray, obscured by rain and fog, like something out of Dickens.

Since we didn't have visas, passports, or seamen's papers, we decided to follow Captain Lothar's advice, which was to remain on the Blackhawk until darkness provided some cover. He also suggested that when we did leave the ship, we hang around a pub called the Speckled Newt, where "lorry drivers lollygagged" while they waited for their lorries to be loaded. Somebody might be going to Edinburgh.

As it turned out that was exactly the case; a man named Nigel was leaving the following morning, and for a price we were welcome to join him. The journey, he informed us, was slightly over three hundred kilometers; we would be there the next afternoon.

Nigel had a room at an inn close by, but as part of the agreed-upon price he allowed us to *kip* in the cab of his lorry. When we retired for the night, it was raining steadily and a cool wind slid off the water, sometimes with enough force to generate a low, ominous moan that brought to mind ghosts locked away in dungeons and high, lonesome towers. So far, England had been a bleak and foreboding place. The temperature hadn't risen out of the fifties; in Detroit it could well be over eighty degrees right now. I hadn't packed warm clothes, not seeing the point. In the cab of the lorry, I wore my only two long-sleeved shirts, and my bathing suit between my underwear and my single pair of long pants. Still I was cold and couldn't sleep. The rain drummed on the metal roof of the cab and poured down the windows, creating a soggy gloom in the muddy parking area, which was lit only by the dim glow of a lone streetlamp. In one of the yards nearby a dog barked intermittently, ending always in a series of mournful whimpers. Why didn't someone let it in? My uncle had bought a bottle of gin from the bartender at the Speckled Newt and he drank from it often as he told me what he knew about Wojtek's time in Scotland, much of which I hadn't heard. Once the company arrived at Winfield Park, Uncle Izzy said, near Berwick-on-Tweed, Wojtek had to be chained up to a special hut that had been built for him. Because there were other military units and small villages close by, it wouldn't do to have him wandering free. With the inactivity, Wojtek grew fat, but he didn't hibernate with the onset of his first real winter. Instead he enjoyed being led around the camp by Piotr or one of the other men, or sitting at the entrance to his hut and observing with fascination the accumulation of snowflakes on the trees and bushes, the fences, the roofs of lorries and camp buildings. As the weeks passed, his fame spread and he attracted many visitors: soldiers from other camps, curious villagers, photographers, and reporters. Members of the Scottish-Polish Society made him a lifelong member. At one point he caused a minor incident when he somehow managed to escape his hut and went walking along the roadside. A lorry driver, a German prisoner-of-war, was so shocked to see the bear out for a stroll that he drove his vehicle off the road, into a pond, and couldn't get it restarted. When Wojtek went to investigate, the horrified driver took off running. Wojtek lumbered along in curious pursuit until the driver scrambled up a tree. The bear had never treed a human being before; what new game was this? For a minute he watched the man, utterly intrigued, then decided to climb up after him. This evoked a series of blood-curdling screams; the German was certain his time had come. Alerted by the screams of imminent death, Piotr, my uncle, and some others ran to the rescue, coaxing Wojtek down with a bottle of beer. Eventually, of course, the company demobilized. Wojtek was left to the care of the Edinburgh Zoo. For weeks the men of the company came to visit and broke every zoo regulation, insisting on crossing the boundaries time and again to play with, and share a beer with, the bear. But soon these men scattered all over the planet to resume their civilian lives. Wojtek found himself a captive of the zoo's brown bear enclosure, in the hands of friendly but unfamiliar zookeepers, who were well intentioned but didn't know quite what to make of the bear. That was all my uncle knew about Wojtek in Scotland. By then his speech had grown slurry and after finishing his story he fell asleep. I was left to the whimpering of the woebegone dog.

At nine o'clock the next morning we were roused by a rap at the window. By nine-thirty Nigel was behind the wheel and we were on the road to Edinburgh. It was still raining off and on, the clouds an advancing fleet of purple and gray reflected in the road water, bloated and woozy, like the whole world had a sickness. After a few miles, a band of salmon-colored sky formed on the horizon, resembling a thick slab of lunchmeat sandwiched between the earth and clouds.

"Look at that," said Nigel, pointing at the ribbon of light. "You might have sun in Edinburgh. A rare occurrence."

The ride had been quiet up to then. Nigel's attempts to engage my uncle had been met with grunts of assent or denial, or the kind of empty response that discouraged further discussion. My uncle was hung over. To fill the silence, Nigel turned on the radio and found a dance hall band; the Guy Lombardo tune recommended enjoying yourself before it's too late.

"What brings you to Edinburgh?" Nigel asked after a few minutes of chipper music, not to be dissuaded. He wore one of those hats with a snap on the brim, pulled low over his forehead. His skin was white as a fish belly.

"I'm seeing an old war buddy," Uncle Izzy said.

"You were in the war? Fighting Jerry?"

My uncle said that he was. Particulars were exchanged; Nigel had also been in the war, a tail-gunner on bombing raids over Germany. He'd been shot down on one occasion.

"That was no bloody picnic, mate. Eight months POW. I wouldn't wish it on anyone."

"I know what you're talking about."

"You were captured too?"

My uncle admitted he was.

"Where'd they stick you?"

"You've never heard of it. It wasn't the Nazis. It was our enemy who became our ally and is our enemy again."

"The Bolshies?"

My uncle nodded.

Nigel slowly shook his head. "May they burn in a red hell of their own making."

"Like you said, it was no bloody picnic."

Uncle Izzy sighed then, and looked out his window at the sodden fields. For a while we rode in silence, except for the jaunty songs coming from Nigel's radio, which felt inappropriate now, like jugglers at a funeral. On a grassy hillside lingered a small herd of cows. They appeared scrawnier than the ones in Ohio.

"Who's this buddy you're seeing?" Nigel asked. "Was

he a prisoner too?"

During the entire drive my uncle hadn't once mentioned Wojtek. I suppose he was worried about Nigel's reaction, or just tired of talking about the soldier bear.

"You could say he's a prisoner now," my uncle said, giving me a look then glancing back out the window.

In the brief second I held his gaze, my eyes implored him to go no further, to resist telling the tale I thought might be forthcoming, where Wojtek steals the cans of peaches from the sleeping soldiers, which would lead of course to Wojtek stealing the panties of the women from the Women's Signal Company, wrapping them around his head, and parading around camp. This story would appeal to Nigel on a number of levels, my uncle might think, and he could have been right *if* Nigel were to believe my uncle. I was afraid he wouldn't, that instead he'd think him a barmy nutter and drop us both off in the piddling rain that had again started falling.

"That's a queer thing to say," Nigel said. "Are you speaking metaphorically?"

My uncle looked at Nigel, then tapped me on the knee. "Do you hear that, Czeslaw? British truck drivers are more intelligent than American truck drivers, wouldn't you say?"

When I nodded, Nigel lifted the corner of his mouth in a smile.

"Look!" he shouted then, pointing out his side window, which he'd just wiped clean of condensation using the sleeve of his jacket.

In the distance, arching from a grove of dark, wind-tossed trees to a point miles away where the landscape escalated into copper hills, was a rainbow. It stood out like neon against the gray-backed sky.

"You'll have the blessings of the fairies," Nigel said. "Your endeavors in Edinburgh will meet with success."

"Good," my uncle told him. "We need all the help we can get."

Nigel dropped us on Princes Street, below the Edinburgh Castle, which perched on its hill above the city like a sooty old owl. Although we were miles from the zoo, my uncle had asked to be driven here; there were things he needed to buy. After Nigel drove off, we strolled down the street, poking our heads in different shops: a kilt and blanket outfitter, a purveyor of shortbread cookies, a liquor store where my uncle bought the cheapest scotch available. From a sidewalk vendor we purchased roast beef sandwiches, then devoured them sitting on a bench in front of an art museum. A man in a kilt played bagpipes next to a puddle reflecting his image. Nigel had been correct; the rain was done for the moment and the sun beamed down, catching the mist that still hung in the air so it glistened like fairy dust. After eating, we continued down Princes Street; then my uncle turned left and led us to King Street, where the shops were more upscale, too upscale for my uncle's liking. He turned down another side street.

"Aha," he said. "Here's what we're looking for."

Douglas Photographic, the sign read. When we walked in, a bell tinkled and a man behind the counter looked up.

"Let me know if I can be of assistance," the man said.

My uncle nodded and started inspecting the cameras, letting the prices guide him until he located the cheapest merchandise.

"What can you tell me about this?" my uncle asked, holding up a beige colored camera.

The man put on his spectacles. "That's an Ilford Advocate," he said. "In some ways comparable to your Kodak Brownie." He opened a drawer and pulled out some pictures, then came over to where we stood. "These were all taken with that camera," he said, handing the photos to my uncle.

They were all snapshots, mostly black and white, of men, women, children, dogs, statues, trains. They all looked pretty good.

"It's a thirty-five millimeter," the man said. "Used to be mine. Note the stove ivory enamel finish."

Uncle Izzy ran his finger over the camera body, then held the camera up and peered through the viewfinder. "How come it's not yours any longer?" he asked.

"I bought the new model. The one your holding is from '49. And you won't find a better price in town, not even down in Leith."

"I'll take it," my uncle said.

After they figured out the exchange rate—Uncle Izzy only had American money—we walked outside with our new purchase. My uncle pulled it from the bag.

"Happy birthday," he said, placing the camera in my hands.

"My birthday was months ago."

"I never bought you anything."

"Comic books."

"That doesn't count."

He was smiling when I finally tore my eyes away from the camera and looked at him. A raindrop slid from a tree leaf and splattered on his forehead. He brushed it away with his knuckle.

"I'll show you how to use it," he said. "Then you need to practice. Tomorrow you'll be shooting Wojtek."

For the rest of the day we knocked around the city and I snapped pictures. There was a festival going on and every street corner in the older part of town had at least one person in a costume. There were princesses, witches, fools, jugglers, mimes, Shakespearean characters, Tommies, pirates, ghosts, lords, ladies, vampires, minstrels. I captured all of them on film and still have some of the pictures. We ended up in a pub, Crazy Man Michael's, where the bartender saw nothing wrong with serving me my first drink, a foamy glass of stout straight from the tap. Once I overcame the fact it tasted nothing like root beer, I enjoyed it, though my uncle took it away before I could experience the full effects. All I felt was mild dizziness and a faraway ringing in the ears, as if I'd rolled down a hill. The bartender told us of a clean place to stay where the price was right, especially if you were a war veteran, and it was there we spent the night, sleeping soundly in comparison to the night before. The next morning I couldn't remember my head even hitting the pillow. I may have been more inebriated than I'd thought.

From the desk clerk that morning, my uncle learned the directions to the Edinburgh Zoo. We made it there in under an hour, changing buses twice under an overcast sky that threatened rain any minute. Everything was green and lush—intensified by the tea-colored clouds that crept across the somber sky—so fresh and alive in the gusting breeze it was almost thrilling. The zoo sat above town on Corstorphine Hill, and as we hiked its well-tended trails looking for the Brown Bear Enclosure, we caught glimpses of where we'd walked yesterday; Edinburgh looked like an enchanted kingdom, its castle on one side, a golden hump of grass thrusting up on the other, the streets below dipping gradually down to the sea.

"That's Leith down there," my uncle said. "Where Mary Queen of Scots arrived from France. You can visit the house where she dined when she got here."

Before we located the soldier bear, Uncle Izzy insisted on visiting the King Penguins.

"They always dress up for visitors."

Luckily, we arrived in time to witness their daily parade and I snapped some pictures. As we made our way up the hill to the bear area, it started to rain. Uncle Izzy put up the umbrella he'd purchased before boarding the bus; he'd also bought ale for Wojtek. From the crest of the hill we had our first look at the bear enclosure. Basically it was a collection of cages with an open area, separated from the viewing public by a moat and a high fence. In the open area there was a pond for the bears to splash around in, and large rocks they could sit or lie down on. Most of the bears were in their cages, but on a long flat rock in the middle of the pond sat one bear not bothered by the inclement weather, who seemed much too engrossed in a group of people on the other side of the fence to be put off by a few raindrops. This bear was quite large. On the rock in front of him he'd stretched out his legs and he was hunched forward slightly, in the direction of his visitors. His ears stuck straight up and were rounded at the top. Unlike the bears in the cages, his fur was light in color, sandy brown, almost dark blonde. His mouth hung partly open.

"That's Wojtek," my uncle said.

It was raining harder, now. When we moved closer we saw the people near the fence were teenagers, only a few years older than me. They wore blue jeans and leather jackets and had their hair slicked back. Other than us, they were the only people still out in the downpour.

"Take some pictures," my uncle said. We were still about twenty yards away. The teenagers hadn't noticed us.

"But it's raining."

"It won't matter."

I pulled out the Ilford and took pictures of Wojtek, then some of the teenagers, who were lighting cigarettes, sometimes two at a time. They tried to throw the cigarettes over the fence to Wojtek; evidently they'd heard he liked them. But none of their cigarettes made it past the moat.

"Blast!" one boy yelled. "Let's see how he likes these."

Out came their lighters and once again projectiles were launched over the prongs of the fence; I thought they'd somehow weighted down their cigarettes because now they were reaching Wojtek. Then they started exploding.

"Hey!" my uncle shouted.

He took off running. By the time they reacted, he'd grabbed the tallest boy by the collar and was mashing his face against the fence. The other three shouted for my uncle to stop and were kicking at his knees and ankles. I stopped taking pictures and ran to help.

"You little shits," Uncle Izzy muttered as he slammed the boy against the shuddering fence, again and again. "You ignorant little shits."

Suddenly he dropped the boy he was holding and swung wildly at the boys who were doing the kicking. His fist found the nose of one of his attackers. There was a dull crunch and the boy cried out in pain. Blood flew from his nose and quickly covered his mouth and chin, his jacket, his pants, the ground.

"It hurts!" the boy yelled, his hand over his nose, blood oozing between his fingers. "It fookin' hurts!"

By now the first boy had recovered enough to get back on his feet. His face was scratched and bleeding too.

"Come on, Mick," he said to the boy with the gushing nose.

Taking Mick by the arm, the boy led him slowly up the hill, followed by the others.

"Bastard!" Mick screamed. "I'll fookin' kill you!"

My uncle was panting. He doubled over to catch his breath.

"I think Wojtek's all right," he said.

His assessment seemed correct. When the firecrackers started exploding, Wojtek had stood up and hopped from one foot to the other, then slid from his rock into the water. Now he was back on the rock, regarding us with curiosity. My uncle, still greedy for breath, slowly straightened up and looked at the bear.

"Hello, Wojtek," he said, waving his hand. "Good to see you, my friend." He placed his other hand on my shoulder. "Say hello to Wojtek."

"Hello, Wojtek," I called out to the bear, imitating my uncle, waving my left hand.

That's how the authorities found us, both of us waving, and Wojtek, for his part, bunching his shoulders and moving his head from side to side, as if trying to see us better. I didn't know whether he recognized my uncle or if it was something he did to everyone. When we heard footsteps behind us, we turned to see two men in uniform walking briskly in our direction: a zoo attendant and a bobby.

"We've had a report of trouble," the zoo attendant said.

"They were throwing firecrackers at Wojtek," my uncle told him. "I stopped them."

"A bit too forcefully," the bobby said. "If what you say is indeed the case."

My uncle stared at him. From under a pair of bushy eyebrows, the policeman squinted back at Uncle Izzy. His face was dotted with red blotches, as if he'd shaved too closely, or was allergic to the starch in his uniform.

"You called the bear Wojtek," the zoo attendant said. "Do you know Wojtek?"

"We were in the same company," my uncle explained. "In the Polish Army."

The two uniformed men looked at each other. The zoo attendant fingered his moustache.

"You'll need to come with us," the policeman said. "None of those kids mentioned firecrackers."

"But I haven't properly said hello to Wojtek."

"Time for that later. We need to sort this through."

He put one hand under my uncle's arm, the other on his wrist, and led us back over the hill towards the main gate. On the way there, my uncle told him where we were from, and what had brought us to see Wojtek.

"A spontaneous birthday gift for my nephew," my uncle said.

"Pretty nice birthday gift."

"Pretty nice nephew."

We were taken to a room in a brick, ivy-covered building, where there was condensation on the windows and a steam heater that wheezed on and off. The room was overly warm and smelled of wet clothing. After taking his raincoat off and sitting behind a typewriter, the policeman typed out my uncle's version of what had happened as my uncle explained it to him, stopping to ask questions when he sought clarification. After he finished, the policeman placed the sheet of paper in front of my uncle. My uncle signed it.

"The trouble is," the bobby said, "your story doesn't remotely resemble theirs. They say you were drinking and picked a fight. For no good reason."

"Where are they?" my uncle demanded. We'd seen two of them when we entered the building, together on a bench in the hall—the two who hadn't been bloodied.

"They were sent home. Two of them went to the hospital first. We have their statement."

"Lies," my uncle said.

"Maybe so," the bobby answered. "But we have no proof one way or the other. You didn't seem drunk. On the other hand, we have no evidence of firecrackers."

"Go out and look why don't you?"

"The zoo people already are. I don't think they'll find anything, though. It's been raining a wee bit if you haven't noticed."

The policeman opened a desk drawer and pulled out a pack of Player's. He lit one and offered them to my uncle, who accepted.

"It doesn't help that you have no passport or visa," the policeman added. "You may be looking at a night in the choky."

"What will happen to Czeslaw?"

"The boy will be looked after."

I didn't like the idea of being separated from my uncle, not one bit. "I took some pictures," I announced. Both men looked at me. The zoo attendant had left a while before; perhaps he was out hunting firecrackers. "If we develop them, maybe we'll see the firecrackers."

My uncle sighed. "That could take days."

"Not if we send the film downtown. We have our own developing lab," the bobby said. "We could have the pictures by morning."

I handed him my camera. After removing the film and arranging to have it picked up by a motorbike messenger, the policeman disappeared into a small office and closed the pebbled-glass door. The afternoon dragged on; it was like waiting outside the principal's office, listening to the murmur of the bobby's voice as he talked on the phone, determining our respective fates. A choky was a jail, I was pretty certain. What lie in store for me I had no idea. Eventually, the zoo attendant returned.

"Did you find the firecrackers?" my uncle asked, rising from his chair.

"No luck, mate. It rained awful hard."

"Of course. Water under the bridge."

My uncle walked to the window. Weak sunlight was now filtering in, exposing motes of dust. It seemed to be clearing up. Shrugging off his raincoat, the zoo attendant tossed it on a bench, then sat in the chair the policeman had occupied. Glancing first at me, then my uncle, he began massaging his moustache.

"Were you one of those bivouacked with him near Berwick-on-Tweed before he came to the zoo?" the zookeeper asked.

"That's right." My uncle stared out the window.

"I probably met you then. You want to spend some time with the old soldier bear, do you? Share a beer for old time's sake?"

"I do." My uncle turned and regarded the zoo attendant.

"Let me have a word with his officialness in there and see what I can do."

When it sounded like the police officer was off the phone, the attendant rapped twice on the office door and disappeared inside. We listened to the rhythms of their voices.

"Don't worry, Czeslaw," my uncle said.

"I'm not worried."

"You'll stay with some nice family tonight. One of the policemen probably."

That's fine, I wanted to tell him but the words wouldn't come. Everything was coming apart, our great plan to reunite with Wojtek and save my uncle disintegrating, and I *was* worried, and also frightened. Nothing had gone as I'd imagined. Perhaps it never would.

"By tomorrow they'll know you're here without Ilona's permission and send you home."

"I won't go."

My uncle smiled. "It's been a good adventure, no? Better than going to Cleveland?"

"I won't leave you."

"I may be going back soon too, if your mother presses charges."

"I'll stay with you 'til then."

"No, Czeslaw. Your mother will want to see you as soon as possible."

I stared at him, still unable to speak.

"This afternoon you'll meet Wojtek. You'll take pictures. You'll have them forever." His eyebrows rose, as if forming a question. *What more can I do?* seemed to be the question.

I felt let down, numb, as if my blood had turned to chocolate pudding. In the past I'd always believed adults held power: they were in charge, forcing me to submit to their wills for reasons I could only vaguely imagine. But the lesson of this trip seemed to deny that. My uncle had no more power than I did. We were both unable to stop the world from spinning in directions we didn't agree with. All my uncle had was experience, which made things easier, but no control, over anything, not even over his own drinking.

"There are condolences," my uncle said. "Fleeting moments of grace."

The sun had reached him; it was brighter now, throwing parallelograms across the parquet floor. He was still tan from the days on the ship, before the rain descended.

"They need to be collected and nourished."

The door opened then. The policeman and zoo attendant reentered the room.

"Wojtek will be fed in half an hour," the attendant said. "You're welcome to join us then."

The attendant opened a locked iron gate and led us down a winding path bordered by bushes and shrubs. We walked in single file—the attendant, Uncle Izzy, the bobby, and me—to the back of Wojtek's cage.

"Wait here while I feed him," the attendant said.

After unlocking the bear's cage, he stepped inside and placed the two buckets containing Wojtek's dinner on the ground. Wojtek had been watching with great interest, and once the zookeeper stepped away the soldier bear immediately lumbered over and began devouring his meal, paying more attention to the bucket filled with fish than the one containing fruits and grass. He ate quickly, stuffing the food in his mouth with his paws, but not ravenously. After every few mouthfuls, he stopped, and as he chewed his food he observed us, wondering, I suppose, who these strange people were watching him eat; usually it was just the zoo attendant. Of course I took pictures. In my pocket were two extra rolls of film and I was determined to use it all, especially in light of my uncle's opinion that I'd be leaving the following morning.

When he finished his dinner, Wojtek sat back and continued to watch us.

"Come here, Izydor," the zookeeper said, who had remained in the cage. "Come say hello to your old army buddy."

When I looked at my uncle, he grinned, without a hint of sarcasm or irony, the likes of which I'd only seen in the pictures Great Aunt Roza shared. "Got your camera ready?" he asked.

I held the Ilford up to my eye and centered him in the viewfinder: my uncle grinning like he was eleven years old, before being invaded by the Soviets, and then the Germans. I snapped the picture.

He took his time walking to the cage, as if he'd just been called to a podium to receive some award, as if it was a ceremony. The smile never left his face. When he approached the bear, Wojtek rolled forward on all fours and sniffed my uncle's feet, then my uncle's crotch. Then the bear stood up, nearly seven feet tall, towering well above my now rather fragile looking uncle, and he gave Uncle Izzy a bear hug.

Snap. Snap. Snap.

Wojtek rocked from side to side, as though dancing with my uncle, my uncle's face lost in the bear's hairy chest; all you could really see of Uncle Izzy were the backs of his legs and the top of his head.

Snap.

"Careful, Wojtek," the attendant called out. "You don't want to crush your visitor."

"I'm fine," my uncle assured us.

Then Wojtek suddenly let go of my uncle and sat on

the floor of the cage, acting very docile. My uncle put his hands on his hips and observed the bear.

"So that's how it is," he said. "Playing teddy bear." Uncle Izzy moved closer to Wojtek. "Kootchie-kootchie," he said, leaning in to scratch the bear under his snout. A sound became discernible, coming from the bear, like a dog might make on being offered a bone. Wojtek licked my uncle's hand.

Snap.

"Kootchie-kootchie-kootchie."

Snap. Snap.

Suddenly Wojtek stood up and put his paws on my uncle's shoulders. Uncle Izzy did the same to Wojtek. For a minute they pushed back and forth, like wrestlers trying to gain an advantage.

Snap.

Since Wojtek was heavier and stronger, he had to be letting Uncle Izzy push him, drawing my uncle in to suit the bear's purposes. Then all at once he had my uncle in another bear hug and sat down with him on the ground.

"You win, Wojtek," my uncle gasped as the bear rolled on top of him.

Snap.

But Wojtek wasn't finished. After a moment he rolled off my uncle. Then he quickly stood up again, and before Uncle Izzy could scramble away, Wojtek grabbed him by the ankles and hoisted him in the air.

"Whoa!" my uncle shouted, now suspended upside down, arms flailing, pockets emptying on the cage floor. "Whoa! Whoa! Whoa!"

Snap. Snap. Snap. Snap. Snap.

"Enough, Wojtek!" the zoo attendant yelled. "Put the poor man down."

Wojtek looked at the zookeeper, then at my uncle, then reached down and scooped my uncle up in his arms, like a fireman saving a victim of smoke inhalation. He proceeded to parade around his cage.

"Very nice, Wojtek," my uncle commented. "Quite adequate lodgings you've found here."

After showing off his living quarters, the bear brought my uncle out to the open area next to his cage, to the edge of the water surrounding the rock we'd found him on that morning.

"No thank you, Wojtek. I've had my bath already," my uncle said, then turned his head in my direction. "Czeslaw, bring me those things I brought for Wojtek before I go for a swim."

I grabbed the bag containing the gifts and hurried into the cage, past the zookeeper, out to where Wojtek was holding my uncle. The bear turned as I approached. I stopped immediately.

"Don't worry. Wojtek won't harm you," the zoo attendant said.

"Take the ale out," my uncle suggested. "Show it to Wojtek."

This I did, waving a brown bottle in the air until Wojtek realized what I was holding. When he did, he took two steps in my direction.

"Put two bottles on the ground," my uncle said. "Then move away."

I followed his instructions. As I backed away, Wojtek carried my uncle over to the bottles and inspected them closely. Seemingly satisfied, he lowered my uncle back to the ground and stood him on his feet.

"So my friend," my uncle said, catching his breath, his face still pink with exertion, "can I interest you in a drink?"

Wojtek looked at my uncle.

"That's a silly question." Pulling a bottle opener from the bag, my uncle popped the caps off the two bottles of ale and placed one in the paw of Wojtek.

"Nazdrowie," he said, but the bear was already guzzling his ale. Wojtek dropped his empty bottle to the ground before my uncle could finish his sip.

"Thirsty," Uncle Izzy concluded. He took another drink from his bottle and offered the rest to Wojtek. Again the bear slurped down the contents and deposited the bottle on the ground. Uncle Izzy opened two more bottles, and then two more, and Wojtek drank almost all of it, until my uncle claimed the last bottle for himself. With his free hand my uncle reached back in the bag and extracted a pack of cigarettes.

"Care for a smoke, old friend?"

Placing the bottle between his knees, my uncle stuck two cigarettes between his lips, setting fire to one, then the other. When he exhaled, the smoke clung to muggy air, forming a plume that turned rosy in the waning sun. Wojtek watched the smoke drift up toward the sky, apparently fascinated. Then the bear looked at my uncle and held out his paw, palm upward. My uncle placed a burning cigarette in Wojtek's paw and for a moment the bear stared at it, then he popped the entire cigarette into his mouth, and I assumed he swallowed it.

"That's some trick," the bobby said, reminding us of his existence. He'd been so quiet I'd forgotten he was there, and about the imminent events his presence implied: my uncle spending the night in jail, me sleeping with strangers and being sent home. For the past thirty minutes Wojtek had made that insignificant; maybe that's what my uncle meant by fleeting moments of grace. And Wojtek had made them possible, an animal without the ability to talk or reason, at least not in the way we think of those things. I felt respect and even envy, not just for Wojtek's ability to adopt certain human behaviors, but for his disinterest in adopting other things: the capacity to deceive, for instance, or wish ill upon another. Perhaps those transgressions were too subtle and complicated for a bear to even notice, but the fact is he remained innocent in their regard, like a child, interested only in what pleased him about human beings and oblivious to our shortcomings.

"Come closer, Czeslaw," my uncle said. "It's time you met Wojtek."

I was still a bit frightened, afraid Wojtek might raise me up by the ankles, as he had my uncle, and drop me in the water. Maybe he associated me with the firecrackers.

"Come on." My uncle took a sip of ale. With his free hand, he beckoned me closer.

I walked over to where he stood, about three feet from Wojtek.

"Shake hands," my uncle instructed.

I took a deep breath and held out my hand.

"This is Czeslaw, Wojtek," Uncle Izzy said, as he took Wojtek's paw and pressed it against my hand. "Czeslaw, this is Wojtek." We didn't actually shake hands, but we touched. His paw felt rough and hardened against the skin of my palm, but warm. Uncle Izzy turned to the zoo attendant. "This is a momentous occasion," he said. "The first meeting of my two best friends in the world."

I don't know how the zoo attendant responded because my eyes were on Wojtek. He had angled his head to observe me better; his brown eyes seemed absent of any awareness other than trust. After a moment, he dropped on all fours.

"He likes you," my uncle said. "He's acting submissive."

True enough. Wojtek arched his back and lowered his snout to the ground, resting it between his paws in the manner of some dogs.

"Rub his head," my uncle instructed, "especially between the ears."

When I did as he suggested, I noticed Wojtek's fur was coarser than it looked, but close to the skin it was soft, where I felt the bone of his skull. Wojtek raised his head but allowed me to continue stroking. I can't describe the comfort it gave: to gain the trust of this animal who had exchanged the life of a bear in the mountains to live among soldiers, and in so doing became lifelong friends with the lot of them.

All too soon, though, the policeman said: "Best be heading back, gentlemen. We're in for more weather." From the east, a shoal of dark clouds was approaching like a black armada.

"One more picture," my uncle said.

The picture I took: my uncle on his tiptoes trying to reach his arm around Wojtek; Wojtek leaning forward to make himself smaller, his shaggy arm draped improbably over my uncle's shoulders. My uncle is smiling. Wojtek's mouth is open too, so you can see his lower teeth, not quite a smile, although I've always thought of it that way. The picture is black and white; all the pictures were that day; but when I look at them now, I recall the brightness of the late afternoon sun before it became an orange smear in the west; and the deep green of the grass in the lengthening shadows of the trees; and the bear smell of Wojtek, and the lingering scent of his salmon dinner; and although I'm probably imagining it from earlier that day, the chirking of penguins that my memory tells me were housed nearby.

The next afternoon I was scheduled for a plane trip to Detroit. That my uncle had predicted just such an eventuality in no way lessened the desolation I felt about boarding that flight. After meeting Wojtek, I felt like I was being forcibly separated from the remarkable bear, and that the likelihood of ever seeing him again was hopelessly remote. The status Wojtek had acquired in my imagination due to my uncle's stories, instead of being dashed by a face-to-face meeting with the shaggy reality, had been reinforced. Thank God I had my rolls of film, which luckily didn't get damaged during the development process back in Detroit. If it weren't for my uncle's foresight in buying the camera, I wouldn't have any record of that afternoon.

But the bigger sorrow of my impending flight was the fact I would be leaving my uncle. We'd grown closer during the journey, he and I, as intimate as any father and son. When we'd returned to the zoo offices after visiting Wojtek, where the bobby had immediately received word that I was in Scotland without my mother's permission, the policeman had called Uncle Izzy a "skiving lowlife son of a bitch."

"There was something I didn't like about you from the get-go," the bobby elaborated. "Besides the fact you're a dumb ass polak."

"You're the dumb ass!" I shouted.

The bobby stared at me.

"He only brought me here because I begged him. I wanted to meet Wojtek."

Raising his eyebrows, the policeman glanced at the zoo attendant, who looked away.

"He loves me," I explained. "That's why we're here. He's my *uncle*." I waited for the policeman to look at me again. "My father's older brother."

When I peeked at Uncle Izzy, he was watching me with a smile.

He spent that night in jail; I spent it in the home of an obliging policeman and his wife who were accustomed to taking in children left temporarily adrift. It fell to these kind people to feed me and keep me occupied until early the following afternoon, when I was to be driven to the airport. But around noon that day, the policeman returned home with some news: first, my photographs had proved there actually were firecrackers and my uncle was innocent in that regard; and second, there'd been a change of plan and I would not be driven to the airport in an hour. I was to remain at their house until later that night, when everything would be made clear.

"Will my uncle be released?"

"We'll see about that."

"How come I'm not leaving now?"

"There's been a change in the flight schedule."

It all seemed rather mysterious. That afternoon I read excerpts from *The Collected Stories of Sherlock Holmes*, and went over in my head, again and again, what I was going to tell my mother when I arrived back in Detroit: it had all been my fault, my uncle had only yielded to my wishes after an unrelenting bombardment on my part.

At ten o'clock that night, I was told to sit on the couch and served a plate of biscuits along with a glass of warm milk mixed with Ovaltine. A half-hour later, there was a knock at the door and Mr. Dale, the policeman, went to answer it. There was conversation in the vestibule, one of the voices was female, and when I looked at Mrs. Dale in her rocking chair, she smiled. By the time the voices grew louder and they rounded the corner into the living room, my heart was pounding.

"Oh, Czeslaw," my mother said, opening her arms.

I jumped up from the couch and stepped into her embrace, returned her hug.

"I'm sorry, Mama."

I'd lost touch with all the carefully phrased words I'd been polishing bright as red apples. "I'm sorry" was all I could say, again and again. She held me so tight I could barely take a breath.

"I thought you were dead—first your father, then

you." She buried the words in my ear.

"No," I said meekly. "I'm here."

"Did he force you to come?"

Pushing away, still holding my arms, she looked at me. There were tears in her eyes. I shook my head no.

"Then why, chlopak?"

"I wanted to meet Wojtek."

"But why didn't you ask me?"

"You would have said no."

She sighed. Her eyes seemed to burn through me. I looked at the floor.

"Look at me, Czeslaw. I know how much that bear means to you. And how much you love your uncle. But you can't just do whatever you want, with no regard for others."

"I'm sorry, Mama."

She pulled me close again. "Look where it's gotten your uncle."

"I didn't mean to hurt you."

She was quiet then, and for the first time I noticed her familiar fragrance—hairspray, facial powder—mingled now with more exotic scents: lipstick and perfume.

"I didn't think I'd get another chance." I spoke the words into the wisps of her hair that tickled my face.

"To see Wojtek?"

"No, to be with Uncle Izzy."

The following morning, my mother, my uncle, and I

went to see Wojtek. Once again, the zookeeper allowed us into the bear's lair, and I took pictures of my mother and uncle with Wojtek. In one snapshot, Wojtek has his paw on my mother's head while her arm is around his waist: best friends. Then my uncle grabbed the Ilford and took shots of me, my mother, and Wojtek. After that it was my mother's turn to snap pictures of my uncle, Wojtek, and me. I don't think I've ever seen her happier, except in some of Great Aunt Roza's old pictures. But my uncle, in those photos, has the air of someone going through the motions. Gone was the joy and abandon of the previous afternoon, replaced by a kind of forced frivolity, a guardedness; his smiles are very close to grimaces. It was sad but not surprising to learn he wouldn't return to Detroit; he'd decided things might work out better in Edinburgh, where he could ship out as a merchant seamen and spend his free time with Wojtek.

"No long faces," he said at the gate to the zoo, which was where we left him. "I'll be back every Christmas. We'll sing carols at Joe Dzirada's Bar."

On the flight back, my mother told me about growing up in Poland, something she rarely talked about. She'd known my father and my uncle since her first day of school. At first, she'd had a crush on my uncle—he was older, a little wilder, radiated a feeling of being charge. After the war, she'd been shocked by the change in him.

"But I still cared for him. Not like for your father, in a romantic way, but like someone who knew all about me and wished only the best for me, the brother I never had. And I felt like I knew him too, inside; I think we are a lot alike. Of course I also knew about his potential. The fact that it never materialized was tragic, but somehow it made me care for him even more."

I told her I knew what she was talking about; I felt that way too.

"I guess I have an odd way of showing it," she said and looked out the airplane window, where the sun was very bright. "I hope you don't think I kicked him out."

I said I didn't think that at all. I knew he made that decision on his own.

When our plane touched down at Willow Run Airport, Aunt Nyusya, my mother's older sister, was there to meet us. By the time we reached Aunt Nyusya's car, my mother had filled her in about the trip to Edinburgh and our meeting with my uncle and Wojtek. Their conversation was light and positive and my mother had already slid into the front seat when Aunt Nyusya said: "One moment, Czeslaw."

I was in the act of opening the back door. I waited as Aunt Nyusya walked around the rear of her Hudson, her high heels rapping the pavement. When she reached me, she bent forward until her face was level with mine.

"Do you know how much that trip cost your mother?"

"No."

I knew it certainly wasn't cheap, and even if it had been, my mother would have had trouble affording it. Everything she earned was set aside for things like the mortgage, monthly expenses, sending me to Our Lady Queen of Martyrs. Aunt Nyusya looked at me as if I perplexed her. Her only son was now in his mid-twenties and perhaps she couldn't decide how to deal with a wayward eleven-year-old; she was out of practice. But she soon reached a decision.

"Don't you *ever* treat your mother like that again," she said.

Her hand was quicker than my reflex to duck. I've never been slapped so hard in my life.

For the next month and a half, until All Saints Day, 1951, I was a prisoner of 111 Ellery Street, grounded for being AWOL in Edinburgh. Over time, though, my mother and I learned to be friends. She accepted that I was no longer her little Czeslaw, and I came to realize that in addition to being my mother, she was also an independent human being, in the same way my uncle was, which is to say she had needs and interests apart from my own, and was not necessarily in the practice of secretly turning cartwheels every time I allowed her into my life.

My photography helped with this. I showed her everything. At first, I think she was just grateful for something we could enjoy together. It wasn't long, though, before she was as thrilled as I was at the photos popping out of my Ilford. In no time she was helping out with my film costs, and for my twelfth birthday she bought me a brand new Zeiss Ikon Contina.

Those cameras saved me. Whenever I felt uncomfortable among groups of people, which was a regular occurrence during adolescence and beyond, I pulled out my camera and started snapping pictures.

"Why do you do that?" my first girlfriend asked before she was my girlfriend.

Normally tongue-tied by direct questions, I answered right away. "I want to make people see things they'd miss if they didn't see my pictures."

"Take one of me," she demanded.

I owe Uncle Izzy for that, though I was never able to thank him in person. Despite many invitations, he didn't show up at our door that Christmas to sing carols at Joe Dzirada's Bar, or any time thereafter. He stayed in Scotland, in Leith near the water, where he was able to sail on the freighters; and when he wasn't on a ship, he was with Wojtek. The two of them became local celebs. On designated days the public was invited to watch the soldier bear wrestle my uncle to the ground, and then lift him up by the ankles. For those occasions, my uncle wore loose-fitting pants with deep pockets so plenty of items could go clattering over the cobblestones: coins, lighters, pocketknives, brass buttons, pens, nuts, bolts, nail clippers. He also organized a reunion between Wojtek and the men of his company, which was sparsely attended but did draw five veterans, much to the delight of the soldier bear. When my uncle went to sea, he never failed to send postcards. I still have the full collection, from ports like Hamburg, Oslo, Lisbon, Barcelona. The final one came from Tunis.

Having a so-so time, the postcard reads. *Sitting in a bar in Souk El Attarine. Would Ilona like some perfume? There's brandy here called Boukha, made from figs, much better idea than fig newtons. WYWH, Izydor.*

A week later my mother received a phone call. Uncle Izzy had missed his ship in Tunis. Beyond that nothing was known. The last people who saw him, two patrons of a café in an old section of town, reported that he left in the company of two Arabs and was noticeably drunk. The police were looking for him but hadn't learned anything yet.

"Something isn't cricket," the caller said, an employee of the shipping firm my uncle had worked for.

"Isn't cricket?" my mother said into the phone.

"I'm afraid your brother-in-law is dead."

My mother looked at me then. "Let's not be hasty," she said to the caller. "This man survived a Russian gulag and served heroically in World War II."

But after two months, when we'd heard nothing more either from or of Uncle Izzy, we had to agree with our caller's assessment and make his fear our own. I suppose Uncle Izzy could have disappeared, deciding to lose himself in a haze of opium and alcohol, but that scenario didn't seem likely. He'd derived too much enjoyment from reuniting with Wojtek, setting his life up to spend time with the bear. Why turn his back on it now?

Genius is the recovery of childhood at will, according to Arthur Rimbaud. I'm no genius and neither was Uncle Izzy, but the things that bring us back to our childhood selves we tend to hold on to, I think. Wojtek did that for my uncle; my uncle died in Tunis.

I saw Wojtek again on one occasion, in 1963. Back then I had a vague notion of doing a coffee table book featuring the bear, but once I returned from Edinburgh I lost the inclination. At the zoo, the attendant from 1951 was no longer there. The new man, Trevor, remembered the stir my uncle had caused though, and allowed me to enter Wojtek's cage for a private meeting. By that time Wojtek spent nearly all his time in the cage, only rarely venturing out from the infrared heat to the open air of the rocks. At first he looked about the same, but then I noticed he moved much more slowly. Sitting and lying down were his primary activities.

"Hello, Wojtek," I said, no longer afraid of being yanked up by the ankles.

He seemed to recognize me, but perhaps I just imagined it. Lying on his side with his head slightly raised, he watched as I approached.

"Do you remember Izydor?" I asked. "Do you remember when I visited you before?"

He gave no sign of acknowledgement, but when I lifted my hand to pet him he lowered his head, as if in acquiescence, and permitted me to do so. I rubbed between his ears as I had twelve years before. His fur was softer now and there was a hoarseness to his breathing, as if he was purring.

"He's falling asleep," Trevor said.

Indeed he was.

I'd brought along a six-pack of ale but left it with Trevor, who promised to share it with Wojtek later, but only in moderation. "He's not much of a hell-raiser these days," Trevor informed me.

Indeed he wasn't.

The following December, back in Detroit, I received a long-distance phone call from Trevor. On December second, Wojtek had died. I was still living with my mother then, in my uncle's old upstairs room, a month away from renting a place of my own from my earnings as a staff photographer. I worked for the Detroit Free Press. The night of Trevor's call I decided to walk down to Joe Dzirada's Bar. The place was decorated up for

Christmas. I found a seat at the end of the bar next to a guy I didn't know. Archie, Joe's son, served me a shot and a beer without asking. Joe, unfortunately, had suffered a stroke. Sometimes he sat at one of the tables, nodding at people, calling everyone "Mildred" or "Archie."

"I used to come here with my uncle," I said to the man next to me.

The man gave me a glance. He looked like a factory worker, in his thirties. The man took a sip of his beer.

"That's nice," he said. "Where's your uncle now?"

"He's dead, I think."

I proceeded to tell him about Uncle Izzy, and about his adventures with Wojtek during World War II. The man watched me with a mixture of boredom and disbelief. I'm sure he thought I was crazy.

"That's very interesting," he said when I was through. "You have a vivid imagination."

"Wait," I said before he could turn away.

Reaching down, I grabbed the folder I'd brought along and plopped it down on the bar.

"I have some pictures."

Made in the USA
Middletown, DE
20 December 2015